"What's that noise?"
Alison murmured sleepily

"Rain." In the darkness Joel stroked her hair, feeling sated but needing to caress her still.

"It doesn't sound like rain," she said languorously.

"For a science teacher, you certainly have trouble identifying natural phenomena."

"Maybe because my senses are all filled up with you." Alison's unthinking declaration brought no response from Joel. Had she revealed too much, too soon? Tentatively she traced the sensual droop of his mouth with her finger. "Why aren't you asleep?"

"Too noisy."

"The rain?"

"Uh-uh. You." He turned into her arms once more. "But don't ever stop talking...."

Shirley Larson 's son, Keith, whom she describes as a "frustrated stand-up comic," inspired this Temptation. The joke about the bear and the flat tire? That's his.

And while Shirley herself is now hooked on stand-up comedy, she has also long been a die-hard jazz fan. For her last birthday her husband gave her the ultimate gift, a state-of-the-art compact disc player. But, of course, there's nothing she's more devoted to than writing. She has also written as Shirley Hart.

Books by Shirley Larson

HARLEQUIN TEMPTATION

HARLEQUIN SUPERROMANCE

Wit and Wisdom

SHIRLEY LARSON

Harlequin Books

TORONTO • NEW YORK • LONDON
AMSTERDAM • PARIS • SYDNEY • HAMBURG
STOCKHOLM • ATHENS • TOKYO • MILAN

Published November 1987

ISBN 0-373-25278-1

Printed in Canada

Prologue

IT WAS JULY, and in the heat of the late afternoon in Iowa, the wet, sweet smell of tasseled corn wafted through the window of Alison Powell's upstairs room. The sun slanted in the west window and played over her shoulder-length red hair, picking up the golden highlights, shadowing the firm mouth and the stubborn tilt of her chin as she moved from her closet to the suitcase on her bed. The aroma of the newly wet ground added its fragrance to the subtle perfume of her freshly showered body, the earthy, outdoor scent filling her with a bittersweet tension and regret that she was leaving. This kind of summer day in Iowa, rain washed, sweet smelling, chock full of ozone, was best enjoyed out of doors. Instead, she was inside packing.

"This isn't like you." Her sister, Diana, leaned against the door frame to deliver her one-liner, her aquamarine eyes a shade lighter than Alison's blue ones and filled with concern.

"I know."

"Women from small towns in Iowa do not run off to New York City to see their lovers."

"I know." Alison went on folding underwear and tucking them into her overnight bag. Diana waltzed into the room, flopped on the bed beside the suitcase and stared up into Alison's face.

"Especially staid, science-teacher types like you."

"I know."

"You're too young for this."

Tiring of the game, Alison drawled, "At twenty-four I'm surely old enough to take my destiny into my own hands."

"Exactly," Diana cried in mock desperation. "You're too old for this." Alison shot her a dry look. Diana tried again. "You may be old enough in years, but you're certainly not in terms of experience. Alison, you're a bright girl, but you're out of your area of expertise here. You're a babe in the woods when it comes to men...." Alison moved back to the closet, her composed face telling Diana she was wasting her breath. The younger woman sighed and took another tack. "One hot summer affair does not a relationship make."

Alison went on folding clothes. "What source of classical literature did you glean that bit of wisdom from, *Aesop's Fables*?"

"Don't be silly. You know I wouldn't be caught dead reading anything so educational. My idea of heavy literature is *Cosmopolitan*, remember?"

"I don't recall seeing anything about a summer affair in last month's issue."

"How could you? You only read *Cosmo* if it's in the bathroom the same time you are. You spend your time with the universal Bobbsey Twins, Isaac Asimov and Nietzsche. And reading them has not, repeat not, prepared you for a dash to New York to confront a man who hasn't called or written you for a month." Diana's eyes widened with mock inspiration. With exaggerated enthusiasm, as if she had never said it before, she cried, "*I* have an idea. Why don't *you* call *him?*"

Alison closed her suitcase with a controlled snap and turned to face her younger sister. "I told you why I don't want to call. I can't see his face over the phone. He could . . . say everything was all right and not mean it, and I would be in the same place I was before, sitting here waiting and wondering and not knowing the truth."

Diana laid her hand between her breasts as if she were saluting the flag. "And being the scientific woman you are, you must have the truth, at all costs."

Alison's blue eyes flashed. "What good does it do to wander around in a dreamworld, living with a lie? I can't go on like this, wondering what has happened, wondering if he—" She broke off. "I've got to see his face. I've got to know what he's thinking, how he feels." She straightened and looked squarely at Diana. "If he . . . if he wants to call it quits, he'll have to tell me in person."

Diana sobered. "You talk as if you're sure that's what he's going to do. Suppose he doesn't. Suppose Joel Brandon looks at you, lifts one eyebrow and says in that Humphrey Bogart imitation he does so well—" Diana tightened her mouth and rasped "—'As long as you're here, baby, you might as well stay awhile?' What will you do then? Give up your teaching job and pour your perfectionist tendencies into being the best groupie any comedian this side of Madison Avenue ever had?"

It was a question Alison had asked herself a hundred times and had never answered. "I don't know what I would do. I'll have to think about that when it happens."

Dismayed that her sister was actually considering living with a man she'd met last summer and really only known a year, Diana tried again. "Are you sure you really love him, Alison? Or is it just that he's the first man who's ever *really* turned you on . . . ?"

Alison shook her head, turning away to pick up a sweater she probably wouldn't need.

"Look, when you met him you were vulnerable; he was caught in rural Iowa and needed amusement. Last summer you were both cautious—at first. But then..." Diana paused delicately. "You, shall we say, threw your bonnet over the windmill?" She paused, her eyes dark with amused teasing. "Has it occurred to you, my cautious sister, caught in the throes of this love affair, that you may be overoptimistic in thinking he's serious about you?"

Her back to Diana, Alison straightened her shoulders. "I suppose it's crazy to think he really does care for me. He's never said that he did." She turned slowly, facing Diana and the truth she had just uttered with characteristic forthrightness.

Hastily Diana rushed in to repair the damage she'd done to her sister's ego, not caring that she was contradicting her own earlier cynicism about Joel Brandon. "Of course he cares for you. Why wouldn't he? You're everything he isn't, a small-town girl who values permanence and stability, a family, values, the whole ball of wax. Didn't you tell me once that he said he felt at peace with himself when he was with you? That's a powerful aphrodisiac you have, lady, that ability to make him feel whole. And after I read that article about him, I can see why he said that. Who would have believed the guy who can walk out onstage and tell jokes with the expertise of Bill Cosby was once a hell-raiser from Brooklyn, so busy rebelling against the military discipline of his four-star-general father that he was ready to blossom into a full-blown juvenile delinquent just to prove his independence? *If* some teacher hadn't spotted his comedic talent and encouraged him, that is." Diana peered at Alison. "If I remember correctly, that article was as much a surprise to you as it was to me. Didn't he ever tell you anything about himself?"

"He . . . never talked about his childhood or his family."

"I rest my case. All the more reason you should wait."

"I can't wait. I've waited too long as it is."

Diana tilted her head. "What we are looking at here is a classic opposites-attract syndrome. Of course—" Diana kept her voice carefully casual "—not that he doesn't have other, more visible assets than a madcap charm. We mustn't forget those big brown eyes and a body that doesn't quit. And hands. Those long, lean fingers look as if they know exactly how to touch a woman." Diana paused, as if awaiting intimate disclosures.

Alison closed her eyes. His hands had known how to touch her. So well. *Oh, so well.*

"All right, so you don't want to divulge any of the juicy details. I'll forgive you . . . for now." Diana's eyes flickered down, and she plucked at her denims, defining a nonexistent crease with her fingers. "Actually, his face isn't too bad, either. It has those masculine, chiseled lines that will only get better as he grows older." She raised her eyes to Alison's. "He's a good-looking man, and you have your own charm. Still, I never did understand how—or why—the two of you got together."

Diana's words dispelled the memory of Joel's lovemaking and brought Alison down to earth with a bump. "I caught him in a weak moment," she said in a wry, self-effacing drawl.

"Hey." Diana came off the bed and put her arm around her sister's shoulders. "I didn't mean . . . I just . . . well, it's such a crazy thing. You're so smooth and organized, and he's such a maker of chaos. I just don't want to see you get hurt."

"It would hurt me more to stay here wondering. . . ."

"I understand." Gently Diana pushed Alison away to look straight into her eyes. "You've got his sister's address as well as his, haven't you?"

"Yes, why? Think I need a port in a storm?"

"It doesn't hurt to know two people in New York instead of just one. Joel might be out when you come calling. Then what will you do?"

"Wait for him."

"You should have no problem with that," Diana said, then muttered, "you've had plenty of practice."

"WELL, NOW THAT YOU'VE WINED and dined me, when are you going to give me the bad news?"

Joel Brandon sat back in his chair and gazed across the hotel dining-room table at Liz Harris, his agent. The elegant blond woman who looked thirty-five and was probably forty toyed with a fork on the snowy-white tablecloth. Joel watched, wondering what she was thinking. They had spent most of the meal politely skirting the subject that had been the purpose of their dinner engagement. When Liz lifted her eyes to return his gaze, her opinion of him—stubborn idiot, naive fool—was written all over her face. Liz was savvy and practical, which was why he'd hired her as his agent. But now he was at odds with her. He didn't have her objectivity. He couldn't. "I can't do a thing unless you agree to—"

"I won't play Girard's club."

Liz lost a bit of her famous patience. "Listen, Don Quixote, you can't right the world's wrongs single-handedly."

"No," Joel drawled, "but I can brighten the corner where I am."

"Then it's no go, Joel. Hasn't this last month shown you anything? Girard has shut you out of every club in town." She reached across the table and closed her hand over Joel's clenched one. "Your career's just beginning to take off. If you refuse to play ball now, you could lose your momentum and drop back into oblivion forever. Girard knows this. He's got everything going for him, and you've got nothing."

A muscle moved on the side of Joel's cheek. "Like Pete."

"What happened to Pete was unfortunate—"

"What happened to Pete was Girard."

Liz let her hand slide away from Joel's and leaned back in her chair. "There's an old saying that you can't cheat an honest man. Pete was open to being corrupted. He didn't have to give Girard all his money—"

"But he did. And now he's broke."

Long ash-blond lashes dropped over Liz's green eyes. "I envy the guy."

That brought Joel's full attention to her. "Why?"

"There isn't a person in the world who cares as much about me as you do about Pete Henson."

"We go back a long way together."

Liz smiled. "The two hoodlums from Brooklyn?"

"Something like that."

"Well—" she picked up her clutch purse "—I wish I had your talent for loyalty, Joel. But I discovered a long time ago that loyalty doesn't pay the bills." Her lovely face was regretful. "It looks as if this is where you and I part company."

He raised an eyebrow. "Deserting the sinking ship, sweet rat?"

"If the sinking ship isn't working, he doesn't need an expensive agent. And if there's one thing I am it's expensive." Her smile held a rueful affection. "You're a special man, Joel. Crazy...but special."

"And you're a special lady," he said, and meant it.

"Thanks." She gathered the light shawl she'd dropped over the back of the chair onto her shoulders and rose.

She turned away from him to leave, hesitated, then turned back. "If you should change your mind, let me know." She leaned over, enveloping him in a cloud of perfume, and kissed him lightly on the cheek. "I suggest you go to California. Give this little contretemps a chance to blow over. Maybe in a year, you'll feel differently—"

"Not in a hundred years."

"Well . . ." Liz straightened, saw the woman standing a few feet away watching them with her heart in her eyes and said in a different, more speculative tone, "Well. Someone you know?"

Joel muttered a curse.

"I see. I think I'd better go."

Joel reached out and grabbed her wrist. "No, stay."

He was acting instinctively, not thinking. He only knew that he didn't want the one woman in his life, the only woman in his life, to be walking toward him now, when a month of bills lay on the hall table of his fifth-floor walk-up apartment and the tattered ends of his career were scattered around his feet.

Alison stood there hesitating, not sure whether she should intrude on him or not. He gave no sign that he recognized her. He felt as if he were in shock, hot and cold at the same time, feeling everything, feeling nothing. There had to be noise in the hotel dining room— there had been a moment ago—but he felt as if he were underwater, where all sound was muted. What was she doing here?

At last, in slow motion, she began to thread her way toward him. When she reached his table, she studied him in that slow, careful way she had. "Hello, Joel." Her eyes moved to Liz, and her thoughts might as well have been written on her face. He knew then why she'd come. She needed reassurance. And she'd found what she thought was betrayal. She said, "I...I've caught you at a bad time."

He looked at the red-gold hair mussed by travel, the correct and proper travelling dress, the soft vulnerability of her mouth, and felt the guilt wash over him in waves. His own stubborn pride and determination to get himself out of the mess he was in before he talked to her had brought her here. He knew exactly how long it had been since he'd called; he'd purposely let the days go by. Now he saw the pain of those uncertain days etched in her eyes, in the mouth she kept under tight control. Her eyes flickered to Liz, and the pain sharpened. Alison thought she was looking at the reason for his silence.

He was filled with guilt and anger and a strange, terrible loneliness. If she believed he was capable of such silly intrigues and lying, she didn't know him at all.

"Aren't you going to introduce me?"

"Liz Harris, Alison Powell." Deliberately, cruelly, he left off Liz's title, even while he slanted a mocking glance at the older woman and wondered if she would supply it.

Her face cool, Liz disengaged her arm from Joel's grip, stepped forward and offered her hand to Alison. "I've heard about you. Hello, nice to meet you. You didn't tell Joel you were coming?" Liz lifted her eyes to

Joel, the message in them clear for him to see. *I don't understand this, but I'll play it your way.*

"I thought I'd surprise him."

Liz arched an eyebrow. "I believe you've succeeded. If you'll excuse me..." She sauntered away, leaving Joel to deal with the chaos he'd created.

"Sit down." He indicated to her the chair across from him, his mouth tightening.

She clutched the back of the chair, and his irritation deepened. She looked like a lion tamer warding off her jungle adversary. "I shouldn't have come."

"No, you probably shouldn't. But now that you're here, I suggest we sit down and discuss your precipitate visit like two civilized people. You look as if I've taken a whip to you."

Normally graceful, she was awkward and ill at ease as she pulled back the heavy chair. Joel cursed himself silently. He could at least be civil to her. "How did you know where to find me?"

"Tracy told me. I called your apartment, and when I didn't get any answer, I called her."

"And helpful sister that she is, she sent you over here straightaway."

She half rose. "I'll leave—"

He caught her wrist just as he'd done Liz's. She stayed on her feet, staring at him, her blue eyes dark. Just having him touch her sent her emotions rioting; he knew that, had known it from the first. Why was it that this woman's reactions triggered that deep response in him that no other woman's ever had? Seeing the effect his touch had on her went to his head like a drug, made him want to touch her more, longer, intimately. He fought to keep his face composed and his voice normal, but he didn't release her wrist. He liked the fragile bones, the feminine softness of her skin under his hand far too much to let her go just then. Now he knew that he'd been starved for the feel of her. "You're here now. You may as well stay. Have you had dinner?"

"I had something on the plane." Her eyes dropped to the place where he held her, and she looked at the wrist he'd shackled as if it were something outside her existence.

"Then perhaps you'd like wine or an after-dinner drink—"

"No, thank you. I couldn't . . . I don't want anything."

His eyes ranged over her, taking in the hectic color in her cheeks. They roamed lower, over her breasts, her waist, her hips, sleekly outlined by the smooth fit of her green cotton dress. "Lucky you." He felt her tremble in response, cursed himself for betraying his need. He'd fallen into such a habit of being honest with her about his desire. Still holding her wrist, he rose. "You're right. It's time we got out of here."

To Alison, Joel looked grim as he walked out into the street, his grip on her arm as relentless as it had been in the hotel. She was carried along beside him as if he were a tidal wave and she mere flotsam. He hailed a taxi with the expertise of a native New Yorker, pushed her rather urgently inside and sat beside her. In the flickering light from the street, his face was like a mask made by a master sculptor, one who knew just how to cut stone to portray haunting beauty in the jut of hard bones against taut skin.

"Joel—"

He turned, and the look in his eyes made the word die on her lips.

"We'll talk when we get to my apartment." His mouth twisted, the action mocking his own words.

Moments later she trudged behind him to the fifth-floor walk-up, her nose rejecting the musty smell. He unlocked the door and stepped back. She preceded him into the room. It was clean but nearly bare. A flowered couch sat pushed up against one wall. Against the opposite wall was the pullout that obviously served as his bed. It was unmade, the sheets a peculiar color of pale yellow, a patch-quilt comforter pushed down at the foot. In the corner was what passed for a kitchen. A stove and a refrigerator with an odd triangular table butted up against the wall, along with one chair.

"Not exactly what you're used to, is it?"

She turned to face him. "It doesn't matter where you live. The only thing that matters is . . ."

"The only thing that matters is who the woman was."

He sounded harsh, derisive, mocking her, as if she had no right to care. Alison stared at him, trying to control her own rising fear and anger. The world had gone crazily awry, as if she were on a merry-go-round and just when she caught a glimpse of something familiar it went spinning away. "You sound as if you're the one who's been wronged."

He took a step toward her, and she moved back instinctively. "Have I wronged you, Alison?" He took another step closer, but this time she held her ground. "All you need are the words, right? All I have to do is concoct an explanation to soothe your wounded pride and I'll be forgiven and you'll fall into my arms."

To Alison, the words sounded right, but they were delivered in such a subacid tone that the biting melody gave the lyric a cutting edge.

He wasn't finished. "Words make everything right. Words like 'I'm sorry,' words like 'It won't happen again.' Those words, my father used to tell me, are the grindstones the wheel of life runs on. Suppose I don't give you the words, my sweet. Suppose I tell you nothing, give you no explanation. What then?"

The reference to his father was the first she'd ever heard. She tried desperately to understand what he was doing. Was he pushing her away because he'd found someone else and he didn't want her intruding on his life in the city? She searched frantically for the truth in his face and eyes and found nothing to comfort her there. "I'm not here to judge you or to ask for words you don't want to say." His eyes flashed with an instant flare of emotion, and she faltered. Steeling herself to go on looking into those brown eyes that seemed to be smoldering, she said, "All I really need to know is that you still—" she took a steadying breath "—you still want me."

"I still want you," he said, in a tone he might have used to tell her he wanted a cup of coffee.

Alison looked at him and ached.

"Don't you believe me? Would you like proof?" Almost as though moving under some power other than his own, he walked to her and pulled her into his arms. When he kissed her, the roughness vanished, blown away by his tenderness, her aching need. His mouth was smooth, as evocative as moonlight and as elusive. The kiss was brief, too brief. And when it was over and he held her away and looked at her, she knew he'd told her goodbye.

"Joel, please . . . let me stay with you." She knew she sounded shameless, utterly without pride, yet she couldn't stop herself from saying the words. Every instinct she had told her he cared for her.

"Stay with me? Lady, look around you. I don't have a bloody dime. And I'm not due to get one soon."

"I could apply for a job here. I can teach here, make enough money for both of us to live on—"

His hands tightened on her arms, and the look on his face told her he was grappling with a need to pull her closer rather than push her away. She hung there, caught on the delicious edge of his indecision. "You make it sound almost...possible. Plausible, even." His mouth twisted. "With just a little help from you, I could become the failure my father always told me I'd be."

Icy panic assailed her. "You wouldn't fail. You'd have time to work on your material, time to take the jobs that would further your career—"

"And feel guilty about every minute I spent away from you."

"You wouldn't—why should you feel guilty?" she cried. "I want to be with you, but I wouldn't expect you to hover over me every minute."

His eyes met hers, the ironic, self-mocking gleam in them chilling her heart. "It wouldn't work. I have things I have to do. Alone." His hands tightened around her arms, and he set her gently away from him. "Go back home to Iowa. Find some nice corn-fed farmer who will give you a home and babies, the things you deserve." His eyes flashed over her in a sudden, perceptive glance that sliced like fire. "The things you want."

"I don't want a home and babies. I want you."

Now his eyes mocked her. "But you can't have me, sweet. A bloody shame, but there it is. True love denied. Now turn yourself around and walk out of this charming little place of mine. You don't belong here." Almost to himself, he said, "I suspected as much. Tonight only proved it." He turned on his heel and went to the corner kitchen, picked up the receiver of the phone sitting on the counter. "I want a cab sent to this address." He rattled it off and then said, "To Kennedy airport. Yes, right away." When he hung up, he turned. His brusque dismissal had drained the color from her cheeks.

The sight of her, her skin whitened with pain, gave him the strength to do what he hadn't had the courage to do a moment ago. Better to hurt her a little now than a lot later. Better to send her away before he succumbed to the temptation to touch the cheek he knew would feel like cool silk. "Look, do I have to draw you a picture? What we had is done, finished, through. The sooner you leave, the better off we'll both be."

"I don't believe that."

"What you believe or don't believe is of little consequence to me. Would you like a drink while you're waiting for your ride?" The offer was made as indifferently as if she were a woman he barely knew and was being polite to only because she was temporarily a guest in his house.

Fatigue and heartsick distress washed over Alison in waves. She wanted to run, to hide, to be alone until the pain that threatened to consume her went away. If it ever would. "No, thank you. I'll go downstairs to wait, if you don't mind."

He stood looking at her for a moment, then turned his back on her and pulled a bottle from the cupboard. She could see the ripple of his shirt across his shoulders as he poured himself a drink, hear the clink of glass against glass. He drank with his back to her, tipping his brown head up to let the the generous proportion of dark amber liquid slide quickly down his throat, his longish hair covering his shirt collar. Standing with his back still to her, he brought the glass down, his head slightly bent. "Well? What are you waiting for, sweet?"

The mocking endearment crawled under her skin and wedged there like a grain of sand, distracted her from realizing that even without turning, he was so aware of her that he knew exactly where she stood.

She wanted to hurt him, needed to hurt him. Yet the words wouldn't come. She looked at the straight back, the dark-brown hair that hung a little too long and a little too full over his collar because he hadn't the time or the money for a haircut, and all she could manage to say was a husky "I was trying to think of a good exit line. I suppose I should say it's been fun."

"Don't say anything you don't mean." He braced his arms against the cupboard as if it pained him to answer her.

"That's your policy, isn't it?" she said to the dark-brown head. "Honesty at all costs."

"I discovered long ago that lying to a woman is far more expensive than telling her the truth. I never lied to you, Alison." His shoulders straightened slightly, but he didn't turn. He kept her locked out of his vision, just as he was keeping her locked out of his life.

"Nor I to you, Joel. And I won't start now. So I can't say it's been fun. Because it hasn't." She pulled the door open.

The sound of it closing behind her reverberated through Joel's head like a cannon shot set off at close range. He turned to look at the empty place where she'd been standing only a few seconds ago, his face dark, ravaged with pain, and raised his glass in a silent toast. "Not bad, Alison." His husky rasp echoed through the bleak apartment, deepening his sense of isolation. "I always suspected you had a flair for drama tucked into a corner of that scientific mind of yours." He raised the glass to his lips and drank deeply, then turned, tossing the remaining liquor from the glass into the sink. He stared at it. "The trouble is...your timing was off. Way off. The wrong time, the wrong place, the wrong man." He rotated slowly to stare at the apartment as if he'd never seen it before. "The only thing that was right was you."

He went to the couch, sank down into the sagging cushion and threw his head back to stare unseeingly at the ceiling, letting the hard, hot pain rise inside him.

1

THREE YEARS LATER, on a steamy June night in New York
City, the cabbie opened the car door for Alison Powell
with a blasé smile. As she looked up at him, orange
neon flashing a club's name, N'yuk N'yuks, played over
her thin, intent face. She thrust a shapely leg from the
cab and stepped onto the sidewalk, her knees unsteady. She was out of her element, too far from home,
and she felt awkward and ill at ease. She was also
plagued with a strong, unrelenting sense of déjà vu.

*Look, do I have to draw you a picture? What we had
is done, finished, through.*

Shutting her mind to that insidious male voice that
she remembered too well and tilting her chin to a stubborn angle, she opened her purse to pull out the bills for
her fare with hands that were shaking. As blasé as the
driver was, he noticed and squinted up at her. His big-
city-bored facade dropped momentarily, and his eyes
took a long, leisurely tour of her. "If you're going in
there, you better loosen up a little. Have a drink. Relax. Life's too short to be taken seriously."

Alison stiffened. It was an old theme, one she'd heard
far too often in the past three years since she'd made that
other disastrous trip to New York. She turned to the

man and favored him with a cool smile. "Life's too short not to be taken seriously."

A flicker of surprise at her unwillingness to be cowed crossed the cabbie's face. With a philosophical shrug he accepted the bill she handed him. "Have it your way, lady."

Alison turned to face the flashing neon, her shoulders straightening. Dear Lord. Was her tension that obvious? She supposed it was.

Anticipation tightened her stomach, made her heightened senses register everything around her. She could feel the moist heat coming from the club, smell the teasing scent of hot pastry being blown into the street by a window fan, breathe in the heavy fragrance of the geraniums in potted tubs sitting on each side of the steps that led down to the door. She was walking into a trap, a lovely, fragrant trap, the path to which was strewn with memories she'd spent three years trying to forget.

A feminine head of dark curls the same shade as Joel's emerged from the shadows, and Tracy Brandon grabbed her arm. "There you are. I was beginning to believe you'd lost your nerve. Hurry up, will you? We're ten minutes late. We'll be lucky if he hasn't already started."

No, thought Alison, they would be lucky if he had started and she could slip into the club unnoticed. She followed Tracy down the short flight of stairs leading to the heavy wooden door, her throat tight.

At the bottom of the stairs, Joel's eyes stared at her from a life-size poster advertising him as the reigning comedian. The Sum of the Parts is More Than Their Equal, it proclaimed. He wasn't handsome, but he had a unique, arresting face, with dark, arching, winged eyebrows that reminded her of a black-caped magician's, a well-cut mouth and a smooth, tight jaw.

He looked exactly the same and yet . . . there was something new in his eyes, a cynical wariness. Behind that practiced lift of the lips, she sensed a weariness, as well. She supposed he had a right to look tired. After a slow, dry time during which he'd worked anywhere and everywhere with very few nights off, he'd clicked on a late-night talk show in California and had returned a year later to take New York by storm. He was enjoying what had been labeled a "meteoric rise to success."

"One heck of a slow meteor," Tracy had grumbled over the phone to Alison a week ago. "He's been working like a dog for years—and now he's an overnight success." He was "hot," Tracy had added. "He's also exhausted. He's in constant demand, and he doesn't turn any of it down. After a performance, he stays up writing new material for his next job. I told him he's going to die laughing." Tracy had chuckled at her own joke, but Alison hadn't been amused. Didn't the idiot have sense enough to take care of himself? No, of course he didn't. He lived life at full tilt, one hundred miles an hour, damn the torpedoes, full speed ahead. Recklessly taking what he wanted and savoring each moment of it— Her mind skidded to a halt and slammed a door on those thoughts. She didn't want to remember what he'd taken with a reckless gleam in his eyes and laughter on his lips.

If Alison had had any doubts about the extent of Joel's success, the wall-to-wall people inside the club instantly dispelled them. It was standing room only tonight for Joel Brandon.

She followed Tracy deeper into the murky darkness that was punctuated by laughter and the sweet-bitter breath of alcohol. Tracy gave her name to the young woman in black tights, abbreviated top and minuscule skirt. The woman nodded and began to thread her way through legs and knees and arms to a spot directly under the stage, where, by some miracle, she conjured up a tiny table for two that bore a Reserved sign. The provocatively dressed cutie snatched the sign away and asked them what they'd like to drink. Alison ordered a gin and tonic, Tracy a fuzzy navel, the newest "in" drink of peach schnapps and orange juice. Anxious to escape the curious and slightly envious glances darting their way at such preferential treatment, Alison dropped into her chair.

A few minutes later the nymph returned with their drinks. Suddenly aware that her throat felt parched, Alison gratefully sipped the cool, stinging gin and tonic.

From the front of the stage, an announcer, dressed like a circus clown in his baggy jeans and suspenders, ended his intro with "And now here's the man you've all been waiting for. Please give a big welcome to Mr. Joel Brandon. . . ."

He wore pleated gray pants and a muted gray-to-rose striped shirt and a narrow tie. Over them he had slung a classically too-big jacket and pushed the sleeves up to his elbows. His understated clothes drew attention away from his long legs and whipcord-lean body and spotlighted his face. His dark hair was cut in a casual style, his brown eyes accented with stage makeup. He looked the picture of poise, but Alison was close enough to see the perspiration already beading his face.

He slipped into his routine as easily as an eel onto ice. One minute ago he hadn't even been onstage; now, a minute later, the crowd was laughing. Alison wasn't laughing. She felt light-headed.

Was it her imagination or had he really given her that slicing, sideways look?

So HIS CHARMING WOMAN FROM THE PAST had come. Joel would have laid odds with any bookie in town that she'd back out at the last minute. She was too close to the stage for him to look at her directly, but he could see her peripherally, see the way she sat stiffly straight at the table. In a white summer dress that left her shoulders bare, her smooth, glistening flesh gleamed in the light spilling from the stage, making him long to see more of her bare skin. He couldn't. Laces like those on a kid's sneaker locked her dress so tightly over her breasts that not a sliver of bare flesh showed through.

But those bare shoulders invited a man's touch. Once he'd been the man to touch her.

Can it, Brandon. You're in the middle of a mono-logue.

Joel strolled to the opposite corner of the stage and went on telling the joke about his father that was half fantasy, half truth, glad he knew the routine so well that he could recite it in his sleep. Thank God Tracy had broken her promise and warned him Alison was going to be here tonight. If he'd simply walked out and found her there looking up at him, he'd have forgotten his name, never mind the monologue.

He hadn't expected the mere sight of her gleaming, amber-gold hair to bring that sharp tug to his gut. He could still remember how it felt rubbing over his skin, like shot silk.

He remembered the first time he'd seen her. He'd been working a small club in Waterloo, Iowa. God, he'd hated that club ... until the night Alison walked in. She'd been with a group of young women, all celebrating their graduation from a teacher's college close by. They had invited him to join them for a drink, and he had.

Out of all the women in the group, Alison had aroused his curiosity. She seemed out of place in the raucous group, almost otherworldly. He'd discovered, as he sat there talking, that she was shy. She was also attracted to him.

"Well, folks, did you ever stop to think about how survival techniques have changed over the years? My father is a master at survival—he's refined it to a science. You ask him something he doesn't want to answer, he just falls asleep. Standing there talking to you, he falls asleep. Let me show you." Joel made a half turn and loosened his tie. When he turned around again, he looked ten years younger. He was a teenager, unsure of himself, his eyes glittering with nervousness, his hands shaking with anxiety. "Dad, can I have the car?" A quick side step, the tie straightened. Before Alison's eyes, Joel became his own middle-aged father. His face deadpan, Joel stood without moving. Then, slowly, with his face positioned in the lights so everyone could see, the lids of his eyes began their agonizingly slow drop and there, on the stage, he began to doze. The audience exploded with laughter. A second later, his eyes snapped open and he was Joel again. "Now I admit it works great for my father, but can you imagine how it must have worked for the caveman boy? 'Hey, Dad, can I have the stonemobile? This big bear is after me—' 'Don't bother me now, son, I'm taking a nap.'" He closed his eyes and let his head loll to one side.

Alison thought, *he's good. He generates a mood, unifies the audience. They're with him every minute, loving him.* He made it easy for them to love him, just as he once had her. . . .

How much later it was that the audience finally allowed him to leave the stage, she couldn't have said. All she knew was that the velvety voice that seemed to be a permanent part of her was saying, "Thank you, all, you've been a marvelous audience. Keep your father awake, don't give a computer an even break and have a good evening." He blew them a kiss and escaped.

Was it easier to breathe because the heat and smoke had cleared, or was it because she'd just been taken off the rack? Alison didn't know. The applause continued loud and strong. Joel bounded out onstage for his second bow, bent lithely, then disappeared.

"I hate to give the devil his due, especially when he's my brother, but he is talented, isn't he?" Tracy asked, beaming.

Alison managed a smile. "Very."

"I told Joel I'd come backstage and talk to him for a minute. Want to finish your drink first?"

Alison shook her head, bracing herself. The sooner she got this meeting over with, the better.

With an odd little look in Alison's direction, Tracy rose and wound her way through the tables toward the back of the stage. She opened a door, and they were in a long hall. Tracy went to the second door on the right, grabbed Alison's arm and marched in.

Straight ahead of her, Joel Brandon stood undressing, his body at an angle to her, one hand on the edge of the makeup table for balance. The blaze of lights ringing the mirror illuminated his profile. He looked as if he'd used up every scrap of energy while he was onstage. Drained of that nervous energy, he was undressing by sheer force of will. His jacket lay flung over a chair, his shirt on top of it. Below that hard, masculine chest, he had one foot raised, his leg most of the way out of his trousers. She caught a glimpse of dark bikini underwear, riding low over a jut of naked hipbone, and a sinewy, hair-sprinkled thigh. Stripped of most of his clothes, the sexual appeal of his body gleamed from every muscular curve.

Arrested, he stared at Alison. As the shock melted from his face, a subtle, more basic emotion reshaped his mouth and wiped away the fatigue. A male arrogance, a careless aggression that said, *Why should I worry about having you see what you've already seen and enjoyed?* Heat rose under her skin, heat and memories and a blaze of emotion she must not show. She'd been right about the new cynicism in his eyes. It was there now, and being exposed to the force of it from across the space of the tiny room was like being thrust under a heat lamp.

For a second and an eternity, he gazed at her. Then, with his brown eyes still fastened to hers, he unhurriedly raised his pants with lazy grace, did up the waist clasp and ran up the zipper. Looking unperturbed, that touch of male aggression as potent as ever, he leaned against the dressing-room counter, his eyes shifting to Tracy. "There's a quaint old American custom. It's called knock before entering."

"Sorry, brother." Tracy didn't sound it. She went to him and planted an apologetic kiss on his cheek. "Next time I'll be ever so discreet."

"That would be a first," he said dryly.

"Aren't you going to say hello to Alison?" Tracy stepped back, her face alive with amusement and interest.

Joel folded his arms and leaned back against the counter. "Hello, Alison." Once he'd looked at her with admiration, warmth and intimacy. The look was gone, washed away by that final hour in his apartment and the intervening years. She felt its loss like a tiny stab of pain. She hadn't expected to regret losing him as a friend.

"Hello, Joel." Meeting Joel's eyes head-on took all the nerve she had. This time, there was no stage to create a buffer between them. Out front, she'd sensed his unwillingness to look at her. That excursion into evasion was over. He was examining her as coolly as if she were a secondhand chair he'd bought at an auction.

Joel's eyes skimmed back to Tracy, his face changing fractionally, smoothing into politeness. "I thought I was going to meet you out front. Are we still going to have a drink together at my place?"

"I've got nothing else to do," Tracy told him.

Never had a woman sounded so complacent about announcing she had nothing to do, Alison thought, wondering how she could have been drawn into the trap so easily.

"Alison doesn't have any plans, either, do you?" Tracy's innocent eyes in her wise face told Alison she'd been maneuvered with real expertise. Alison fought the urge to clench her teeth. Tracy had said nothing to her about a tête-à-tête with Joel after the show.

While Alison tried to think of a way to escape this cozy threesome, Joel turned his back to her and smoothed cream on his face as casually as if he were accustomed to having an audience of admiring females watch him remove his makeup. "Perhaps she does have plans." His eyes met Alison's in the mirror while he waited for her response. In that mirror image lay a host of emotions. Fatigue was there, mingled with a strange, vulnerable pride. *Go ahead, refuse, if that's what you want to do*, his eyes seemed to say.

His pride drew out hers. If he could be indifferent, so could she. She lifted her chin. "I have no other plans."

"I'm glad to hear it." Joel's expression in the mirror was carefully casual, his skin pulling along his jaw as he wiped the cream away. He broke eye contact with her, searching for something on top of the counter in front of him. His hands closed over a set of keys. He turned, his arm came up and the keys went flying through the air at Tracy in a gesture so quick and smooth that Alison jumped. Tracy caught them, obviously used to her brother's lightning changes of mood.

"Go on ahead. I'll catch up with you." Joel raised his eyes to Alison's in the mirror. His face bare and shiny from the cream, he looked arrogantly masculine and still . . . strangely vulnerable. As if he realized that, his eyes flickered away as though he were no longer interested in her. "You will excuse me while I shower and change?"

"Take your time, brother," Tracy told him airily. "I'll fix Alison something tall and cool while we're waiting. I know where you keep the good stuff."

"Sure," Joel said to Tracy, his eyes on Alison. "Make yourself at home."

A few minutes later, in the taxi they'd found outside the club, Tracy turned toward Alison, a worried frown pulling her brows together. "You don't think the publicity is turning his head, do you? He was rather...cool toward you."

Alison didn't answer immediately. Instead she turned away from Tracy and sat watching the blur of lights flow alongside the cab. "Why shouldn't he be cool to me? We are strangers, after all."

"Joel never told me what happened. I suppose you won't, either."

"It isn't important now."

"I thought maybe—Joel means a lot to me." Tracy stared out the window of the taxi. "I suppose you know his childhood wasn't exactly ideal. Dad was so hard on him. He wanted him to be a perfect man. He expected him to excel in everything he did. Me, Daddy just doted on. But he expected Joel to be Superman. The funny part of it is Joel nearly succeeded. He was bright, and he was a good athlete. But the year he was sixteen Dad began to be even more critical. Their relationship deteriorated, and Joel began to rebel. It was a terrible year." She turned and looked at Alison. "I tried to run interference between Dad and Joel, but by that time there was no talking to either of them. They made it impossible for me to stay neutral. I chose Joel. Dad had Mother; Joel had no one. I wanted him to be happy. I would give him the world if I could. You were so good for him in those early days. He came back from Iowa the summer you met and was so happy that I—" She broke off. "That's why I...I always wanted you two to get together. There's no chance that this time you might—"

"No," Alison said quickly, firmly. "No chance at all."

A sigh issued from the other side of the cab. "I worry about him. He's burning the candle at both ends, and despite what the poem says, on him the light is not so lovely. He's beginning to look ragged around the edges."

"I hadn't noticed that his edges looked all that bad," Alison murmured.

"You mean he looks good to you?" Tracy looked childishly eager.

Alison refused to rise to the bait. "He's a good-looking man," she said in a matter-of-fact tone. "It runs in the family."

"Thank you." Tracy fiddled with the handle of her purse. "He is doing well. You should see his new place. Well, you will in a minute." Tracy lapsed into silence, and so did Alison, not knowing what to say. Her own thoughts and feelings were too muddled. She'd kept in touch with Tracy, mostly because Tracy had insisted. On that last, fatal visit to New York City, she'd grown to like Tracy. Knowing something had gone wrong but refusing to acknowledge that her brother and her new-found friend were no longer together, Tracy had written to Alison feverishly, answering her friend's every letter immediately. If Alison let too much time elapse between letters, Tracy called to ask if she was all right.

For Tracy's sake, she had to get through this evening as gracefully and as unemotionally as it was humanly possible to do. She was going to sit for a few minutes in the place where Joel lived, drink one helping of Joel's liquor, and then she was going to walk out of his life as quickly as she'd walked into it.

Joel's apartment told her that he was richer and more successful than she'd thought a man could get telling funny stories. The luxurious condominium on the fifteenth story of a new building overlooking the Long Island Sound oozed comfort and money. It was in complete contrast to that poor, fifth-floor walk-up she'd once stood in. Here she was in danger of drowning in the rug. Expensive wallpaper, a delicate gold outlining fern leaves, covered the walls. Drapes made of a light crepe de chine hung gracefully at the windows. Everything was done in exquisite, expensive taste, yet she had a sudden, nostalgic pang for that dingy apartment with its rumpled bed and quilted comforter. These living quarters—and that was what they were and nothing more—had a cool, programmed look that made her feel she'd walked into an asexual dwelling where no real human being resided. There was nothing of Joel here, no mementos, no knickknacks. The kidney-shaped coffee table and the mantel were bare. She thought of her own snug apartment in Iowa filled with the clutter of her work, dried maple and oak leaves she was cataloguing covering the coffee table, crushed rose petals smelling cinnamony and sweet in a glass potpourri jar, and the Have a Happy Summer, Miss Powell signs her students had made spread all over the floor so that she could see each one. She, at least, had her pupils. Joel, it appeared, had no one. Guilt, raw and harsh, tugged at her conscience. Yet surely their aborted love affair hadn't caused the cynicism, the distancing, she saw here. She had been like a pebble tossed into the pool of his life, quickly sinking out of sight. Perhaps it was his rise to fame that had changed him. It had to be.

She didn't want the intimacy of being in his abode when he wasn't there. It told her too much about him, things she didn't want to know. It gave her too clear a picture of his life, told her that he'd accepted his status yet was rejecting it, that he was successful, wealthy, in demand...and lonely. Lonely and weary. Tracy hadn't exaggerated about his health. There had been a deep, bone-tired fatigue in those guarded brown eyes. That tiredness tugged at her, made her want to go to him, touch him, soothe him, as she had once....

Searching for a distraction from the thoughts that haunted her, Alison walked to the window wall at the far end of the room and pushed aside the drape. Lights twinkled in a thousand pinpoint stars, cars flowed over the streets, the water gleamed silvery pink in the glow of streetlights. Joel had the city at his feet in more ways than one. Surely the spectacular view would offer him solace, if he relaxed long enough to allow it. She wondered if he did.

She turned again, casting a more critical eye over the decor. The room was done in shades of turquoise, blues and greens that reminded her of the ocean. "I have an affinity for water," he'd told her once, when they'd stood looking out over the tiny lake near her hometown. "Water offers a man infinite variety...just as a woman does...."

Tracy broke into her thoughts. "He has maid service and a cook, but I'd take either one of their jobs in a minute. He's never here, he's on the road so much crisscrossing the country, going from one one-night stand to another. He does most of his writing in airport terminals." Tracy dropped the keys on the counter that opened into the dining alcove from the kitchen. "This is a long way from the place he had in the Village, in more ways than one. Sit down." She ran lightly up the two steps to the dining room and disappeared around a corner. Disobeying her, Alison stayed where she was, listening to the clinking of glasses as Tracy fixed their drinks. The sound seemed to intensify the silence of the rooms.

"The view does draw a person, doesn't it?" Tracy said when she came toward Alison a few minutes later, holding out the glass of gin and tonic. "I wonder if Joel ever takes the time to appreciate what he's got here. Probably not." As Alison took the glass, Tracy's eyes flickered over her and away. "My guess is he lost you that way, by not appreciating what he had in you."

What had happened between her and Joel was the last thing Alison wanted to talk about. She cradled the drink in her hands and turned from Tracy to stare out at the darkness. "If I'd known you were going to dredge up a lot of ancient history, I would never have come to see you."

"Nonsense. Of course you would have. You were as curious to see Joel as he was to see you— Oops. I wasn't supposed to let that particular cat out of the bag."

Alison turned to Tracy, one brow lifting. "It just slipped out, is that it?"

Tracy gave Alison a bland look. "Are you accusing me of subterfuge?"

"Yes—"

The buzz of a telephone sounded in the room. "Saved by the bell," Tracy murmured, making a graceful turn to set her glass on the coffee table. The recorder sitting on the end table clicked on. Joel's voice made a quip about electronic helpers and asked if the caller would leave name and number. "This is Evan Brody," a masculine voice said. "I was told I could reach Tracy Brandon at this number—"

Tracy flew for the recorder, punched a button and said breathlessly, "Evan? I'm here...."

Alison turned away, wanting to give Tracy some privacy. Evan was the new man in her life and possibly the most important one to date.

From behind her, Tracy said, "Alison?" Alison turned to see Tracy sitting on the sofa, her hand over the phone, her face alight. "Evan wants me to meet him at the Hyatt. I told him you were here and we were going to wait for Joel. Shall I say an hour?"

"There's no need for you to wait."

"Are you sure? I wouldn't put you in an awkward spot like this on purpose, Alison, really."

Alison reached for strength inside herself and discovered to her relief that it was there. "Will you stop? You make it sound as if I can't spend a few minutes with Joel. I assure you, I can."

Tracy seemed to pause for a moment. "I suppose it doesn't really matter. After tomorrow, you'll be off in the wilds of the Adirondacks, where you'll be safe from—"

Alison raised a brow. "Safe from what?"

Tracy shrugged. "From civilized man. If you're sure you don't mind—"

"I don't mind," Alison told her emphatically, thinking it was Joel who would probably mind seeing her without the buffer of Tracy's exuberance.

Tracy turned back to the phone, and when she had murmured her acceptance and stood up to go, Alison's mouth curved in a smile. "Must be a special guy. He says 'Jump' and you jump."

"He is special, very much so."

"Well, don't just stand there. Call a cab and get going."

A few minutes later Tracy was gone. The apartment seemed quiet without her breathless presence. Quiet. Undisturbed. Detached. Remote. Holding her glass, Alison walked to the window again. From here, Joel could look out at the world and not be a part of it. He could be a spectator and not a participant. Was that what he wanted? Was objectivity what he looked for when he wasn't standing on a stage making people laugh? Or did he deal with life by laughing at it?

In the silence of the apartment the phone rang. The recorder clicked on; Joel's voice filled the room. The beep, a pause, and then a feminine voice, low, husky, said, "Joel? Give me a call when you come in." Another click, and the caller was gone. The woman had known Joel would recognize her voice and hadn't bothered to leave a name or a number.

The second woman who phoned had a bubbly laugh and wasn't quite so sure of herself. She left her name and number and said she hoped Joel wouldn't be too tired when he got home from the club to return her call.

The third woman's name was Helen, and she had just enough of a European accent to make her sound exotic and lovely. When Helen reminded Joel about what a wonderful time they'd had together that Monday night a few weeks ago, Alison collected her purse and sprang to her feet. What a fool she'd been, imagining him alone and lonely, like a haunted prince in his castle. He had so much female company panting to be with him that he needed to stack them up in approach loops like descending airplanes.

She jerked opened the apartment door and nearly knocked Joel down. He looked as surprised as she. "Alison? What's the matter?"

"Your sister's gone to keep a late date, and I—I was just leaving." She stepped back, making room for Joel to walk in. Simple movements, normal movements, movements people made for one another. "I was on my way out."

"You waited until I got here...but now you're going?" If anything, he looked more finely drawn than he had in the dressing room. Devoid of makeup, the beginnings of a beard on his jaw, his face lacked color and life. He had always moved with a lithe grace, but now, as he came inside, closed the door behind him and slouched against it, effectively cutting off her path of escape, he seemed to be holding himself erect by sheer effort of will. "Surely you can stay for a few minutes— Damn it, don't look at me that way. We're not strangers."

"Yes, we are," she said, knowing it was true.

"Once upon a time, we weren't." His lean body outlined by the soft, dark wood, he was all male, sure of himself on his own turf. Those brown eyes moved lazily over her, making her aware of their isolation together in the quiet room, his fatigue giving his mouth an erotic droop. "Once we knew each other very well."

"Once upon a time. Long ago and far away. Fairy-tale stuff—"

He made a muffled sound in his throat and reached for her. "Stop distancing me with those cool words and that cool look and that damn dress. I'm tired of listening to your charming little defenses, tired of telling myself I can't touch you." He captured her arm with one hand while his other hand came up to her chest. She felt the sharp tug on the lace of her dress, shocking, intimate and exciting. Far too exciting. She made a move as if to escape, but his fingers tightened on her arm and his eyes, darkly near, warned her not to lie about what she was feeling. The cotton tie sang through the loop, and the end of the string dangled free while those dark eyes of his never left hers. "I've forgotten," he murmured, his voice close and silky, "how much fun it is to surprise the cool, unflappable Miss Powell."

She made another restless movement, but he kept her locked in place. Those warm fingers on her arm were a hundred different things at once, evocative, remembered, bringing old feelings to life, feelings she hadn't expected to feel, didn't want to feel.

He hooked a finger under the last loop and, with one easy move, drew it loose. The material gave, and the narrow, silken valley of tanned flesh between her breasts gleamed through the white cloth. She said coolly, "In the last five minutes, three women called for you."

Just as coolly, he stood gazing at her for a moment. Then he shrugged. Almost as if he didn't realize what he was doing, he dragged a lazy finger over the very top of the breasts he'd exposed. Under his touch, her skin burned. She stood unmoving beneath his caress, struggling to achieve the same blasé disregard for that marauding fingertip as he was giving it. His eyes captured and held hers, a shrewd look of understanding lighting their depths. "Is that why you were running out of here as if the hounds of hell were after you, because you didn't care for the competition?"

"I withdrew from the race a long time ago."

A slow, lazy smile lifted his lips. "But you're here now. Have you come to put yourself back in the race?"

How well she remembered that disarming charm. Joel Brandon was one of the most dangerous of the male breed. That smile, unsheathed, was a lethal weapon that both disarmed and enslaved a woman. "Not at all. So you see, the sooner I go, the sooner you can answer your calls—"

She moved to walk around him, but he dragged his hand away from the top of her breast and caught her by both arms. "You're not really planning on leaving."

"Yes," she said steadily, "I am."

His eyes mocked her gently, but she caught a flicker of compassion there. "Yes, I suppose you are." He sounded resigned and weary again. He loosened his hold, then shook his head. "Wait a minute. You can't go out on the streets of New York looking like a walking invitation to trouble." Casually, as if she were his daughter, he caught the laces he'd loosened and redid them into a tidy bow, his eyes on the job he was doing. "Tracy tells me you've landed a plum job this summer up in the Adirondacks, teaching kids how to tell wisteria vines from poison ivy." He adjusted the length of one of the strings, tugging one to match it with the other. "Is that right?"

She didn't know whether he was talking about the way he'd tied her dress or his statement about her summer job. He still wasn't looking directly at her.

"I have a teaching job at a science day camp, yes."

He stepped back a pace, his eyes moving lazily over her. "How like you to find a summer job. Not a moment must be wasted."

"I like to keep busy."

"Busy, involved, intense Alison. You'd better have a care. There might be wolves in those mountains."

"There are no wolves—"

"I was talking about the two-legged kind."

"You mean the kind that are indigenous to both country and city?" She gazed steadily at him.

He smiled, appreciating her counterthrust. Joel had always encouraged her to answer him in kind. He'd taught her to talk without thinking, among other things. "Are you saying I'm a member of the species?"

"If the shoe fits—"

"The shoe doesn't fit, Alison."

Amazed to see the light of amusement fade from his eyes, Alison was suddenly alert and guarded. He was serious. She thought about walking away from this argument, just as she had from the other one they'd had three years ago. But no, she wasn't going to walk away, not this time. "Twenty minutes ago, before your phone recorder started suffering from burnout, I might have believed you."

"You think I'm lying, the same way you thought I lied to you three years ago." He gazed at her, his eyes steadfast.

She hadn't meant to discuss what had happened. "It doesn't matter. It's too long ago to worry about."

"Is it?" he drawled.

"Yes, it is," she insisted, his persistence making her eyes go bright with temper. "Let's just . . . forget it."

He found it interesting that she was angry. He wanted badly to touch the heated silk of her cheek, to see if it was as smooth and pearly under his fingers as it looked. The truth came from his lips, a truth he'd been unwilling to say that night. "She was my agent, Alison."

She met his gaze steadily, her eyes clear. "It didn't matter who she was. What mattered was that you wanted out." Her chin came up to that little stubborn angle he remembered well, had even imitated on occasion.

"Was I that obvious?"

"Painfully so." She tried a careless smile, but she didn't quite pull it off. To Joel, she looked like a determined fawn, poised for escape at the edge of the forest. He leaned away from her, giving her space, wondering why it bothered him that once he had hurt her very badly.

"Don't lose sleep over it, Joel. I considered it a learning experience, cheap at half the price."

"What did you learn?" Hooded brown eyes watched her.

"I learned I didn't want what you had to offer. We're too different, you and I."

Shaken by her words, he stared at her, wondering why it had taken all this time to get to the truth. He'd thought the break between them had been related to trust, that she hadn't trusted him and he'd been too proud to apologize for something he hadn't done. And too proud to come to her as a penniless comedian. A joke. "I thought you liked my lighthearted, devil-may-care approach to life."

"I did at first, but—"

"The luster began to pall. But you, being a conscientious lady, were trying to keep it going by coming to see me. How thoughtful. My being with Liz at that moment wasn't a tragedy, it was a heaven-sent opportunity for you to break things off, wasn't it?" Strange how angry that made him feel when it had happened so long ago. Tired as he was, feeling more than a little betrayed, he forced himself to think. She wasn't going to walk away from him so easily this time, not if he had his way. And over the years that they'd been separated, he'd learned how to get his way. "And what about now, Alison? Why did you come to New York?"

"I came to see Tracy—"

He said a rude word that encapsulated what he thought of that lie, grasped her shoulders and turned her so that her back was to the door. His hands were hard, demanding, on her shoulders. It was a new sensation, to be manhandled by Joel. She should have been frightened. It was more frightening that she wasn't. Her nerves danced with wild, restless excitement that she hadn't felt for three years. He said, "We're both adults and over the age of consent. And unlike that day three years ago when you made your reckless and uncharacteristic descent on me, I now have something to offer you financially. I'm willing . . . and able . . . to give you what you wanted then." His eyes were opaque, his face unreadable.

Forcing her expression to show nothing of what she was feeling, she said coolly, "What are you saying?"

He smiled at her as if she were a child who was being purposely difficult. "I'm asking you to move in with me."

His tone was so dispassionate she felt as if he'd slapped her. His words were an arrogant acknowledgment that the sexual attraction between them was as strong as ever, that he didn't care that there was nothing else. "Just like . . . that?"

"Just like that." His dark-brown eyes met hers steadily.

"There's . . . nothing between us now."

He let the silence build with the ease of a professional. An eternity passed before he said in a soft voice, "Liar."

She shook her head, searching for words that would reach behind that cynical facade. "I don't understand why you would want such a thing."

His eyes passed slowly over her face and then downward, taking in the slim line of her throat, the curves of her breasts just visible above her dress, the feminine

thrust of them against the white cotton. "Then you have less imagination and intelligence than I remember you having."

She tried desperately to read his expression, tried to find something of that wild, uninhibited but caring man she had once loved. There was nothing she recognized in his eyes or face. He was a stranger, a cynical stranger. "You must be joking."

"Nowadays I save my jokes for the stage. Look around you, sweet. Surely you can see I'm much more able to afford you than I was three years ago." Under the subtle mockery, there was steel, new steel honed in the heat of his long struggle for success, steel that she'd never heard in his voice before. At thirty-four Joel had learned, in the rough-and-tumble world he inhabited, to go after what he wanted. And tonight, for some reason she couldn't fathom, he wanted her, so much that he was willing to try to buy her. The invitation was there, in his eyes, his mouth, his body.

He was close, too close, his body almost but not quite touching hers. She was locked between him and the door, and she could feel the heat and warmth of him, see the lazy, sensual droop of his lips. And for one glorious moment she let herself think what it would be like to say yes, to let those lips melt with their remembered warmth over hers, to feel the touch of his hands, to know the mastery of his body, to have the right to touch him again. She'd been keeping that need at bay ever since he'd walked onto that stage. But if she tossed away her misgivings and stayed to take what she wanted, she would have to touch him as he touched her, without

love. She would have to look up at those cynical eyes hovering over her and pretend she was as cynical as he. She knew she couldn't do that. He was an actor; she was not. He would look at her and see her heart in her eyes and know that she still loved him. "I can't stay, Joel."

"Can't? Or won't?"

Her chin came up a little. "Won't."

"Is that a no?" At her nod, he smiled and shrugged. Slowly, slowly, so slowly it felt as if he were taking her soul with her, he slid his hands down her arms and released her. "If at first you don't succeed, try, try again." He shook his head, a rueful smile coming to his lips. "God, I must be tired. Platitudes aren't my usual fare. Doesn't the thought of comforting a tired old man appeal just a little to that compassionate nature of yours?"

Her eyes went to the phone recorder, where the light still shone, indicating he'd had callers. "Why bother with me when you have many other . . . opportunities for amusement?"

He stared at her for a moment, seemingly about to argue. "I don't suppose there's any hope of you letting me see you back to Tracy's apartment?"

How many men would have wanted to take her home after she'd just told them no? Only those with Joel's sense of humor. "That isn't a very good idea—" a tiny gleam flickered in her eyes "—when you have so many calls to return."

He turned away from her, shielding his expression from her gaze. "The only call I'm going to make is for your cab. You will let me do that much for you? For old times' sake?"

There was a touch of irony in his tone that disturbed her. "If you like."

LATER, WHEN ALISON HAD GONE, Joel was left in an apartment that echoed with emptiness. He muttered a curse and went into his bedroom, tugging at the buttons of his shirt with the frustration of a man pushed to his limit. Shirt open, shoes on, he sprawled on his back on his water bed, his eyes on the golden, empty glow of the lamp brightening the so-correct beige ceiling. He was alone. Again. The subtle wave of the water under him gave him a sudden, swift impatience for the world and its riches. He had everything that money could buy, except the one thing he wanted most. He had tried to buy her, but she wasn't to be bought.

Or was she? Perhaps she was. Not bought in the strictest sense of the word, but bought because his money could put him in her realm. If she wouldn't stay with him, he could go to her....

Pride whispered to him to forget the wild scheme that was siphoning up from the bottom of his creative mind. Need urged him to act on the plan that was even now becoming more and more feasible.

Mentally he ran through his schedule for the next two weeks. Another two nights at N'yuk N'yuks, a *Tonight Show* appearance, a television game show. Nothing there that couldn't be canceled. When was that taping for the comedy special? If he remembered correctly, not till September. By that time, he would have been successful with Alison...or have suffered the most humiliating defeat of his life.

No risk, no glory. He could stay safe . . . or he could take the big gamble.

Moving with a sudden, quick energy, Joel rolled over, reached for his bedside phone and punched out a number. He lay back again, fighting his fatigue with the anticipation that fired his blood. He was playing a long shot. But he was a gambler by nature. He'd gambled on his career and won. Now he was ready to try for bigger stakes. He wanted Alison again; he wanted her in his bed. And he was accustomed to getting what he wanted.

When a male voice on the other end of the line said hello, Joel answered. "Ted? Listen, I've decided I want to get away for a while. Clear my schedule for a couple of weeks, will you? And find me a club to play up in the Adirondacks. The Saranac Lakes area around Tupper. I want to spend a few weeks in the mountains."

Automatically he held the phone away from his ear, waiting for the explosion to subside. Then he said, "All right, so all they have up there are biker bars where the guys wear leather jackets and tattoos. I'll buy a leather jacket and act like I have a tattoo in a place where nobody can see it."

He held the phone away again briefly, then cradled it to his ear. "How do *I* know where these places are? That's your job. Oh, and, Ted—have it done by tomorrow, will you?" Quietly, deliberately, he hung up, switched off the phone bell and rolled over. In seconds he was asleep.

2

THE INSIDE OF THE LITTLE GRAY TOYOTA that had seemed comfortable a few hours ago was beginning to feel like a cage. Apprehension had followed Alison out of New York City to the airport, wound around her like plastic wrap when she'd landed in Syracuse and stuck like glue when she'd climbed into the rental car. Her encounter with Joel hadn't gone at all the way she had envisioned it would.

The man was dangerous, more dangerous than she'd remembered. Or had he changed that much? She steadied the wheel with one hand and propped an elbow on the open windowsill, straightening her spine to remove yet another kink, and felt her hair tangle in the cool breeze. This soft, summer night reminded her of the one when Joel had come from New York City, wired, restless. Out on an evening stroll with her, he had given in to an impulse to shinny up the creaky ladder plastered to the side of the water tower in her small town. At the top, he'd hung against the rail and dared her to come up after him. Her heart in her mouth, she hadn't gone.

Why was it that whenever she was feeling uncomfortable about herself, wondering if she'd done the right thing, that memory surfaced?

Alison plucked a swath of red-gold hair off her cheek. Tracy had been alive with curiosity that morning, but she hadn't asked any questions. In the afternoon, at the airport, those questions lingered like smoke between them, but when Alison turned to tell Tracy goodbye, the other woman had simply hugged her and told her not to stay away so long the next time.

There wouldn't be a next time for her and Joel. She would never see him again.

She drove through the dark, still town of Tupper, casting an anxious look at the gas indicator riding close to empty. When she'd finally realized she should have been looking for a gas station, she hadn't found one open.

She would be glad to get to the camp and settle in. Eve Cunningham, the camp director, had assured her that her cabin would be ready when she got there.

Alison reached the turnoff, swung into a curving lane and came out into the clearing where the buildings were clustered. One lone gas lamp illuminated the larger cabin where the dining hall and the classrooms were located. Behind this building, close to the woods, stood a ring of smaller cabins. Was it her imagination, or did the cabin assigned to her seem more deeply set in the woods than the others?

Not far from the cabin, the glimmer of the lake sparkled in the moonlight. Tonight the water was pool still, as tinfoil bright as an artist's painting. Only the faintest whisper of a breeze rustled through the long-needled evergreens, and from a distance an owl cried, the sound eerily magnified by the still water.

As Alison got out of the car, a cool wisp of wind drifted over her damp arms, heightening the chill on her flesh. Shrugging her shoulders to release her apprehension, she went around to the trunk to get her suitcase.

She walked up the steps to the porch and saw that a shaded lamp, the kind that hung from a cord in the ceiling, swung over the kitchen table, giving off a muted glow. Someone had turned that lamp on . . . someone who was still inside.

Pottery clattered to the floor, shattering. A curse in a low, masculine voice followed.

Every instinct told Alison to run. But another, cooler part of her brain told her the intruder had to be connected to the camp. Burglars were not ordinarily so clumsy and vocal. She moved closer to the door, stepping into the pool of light. As she did so, the figure inside the cottage melted back into the shadows. Her body chill deepened, feathering along her spine. She had identified the figure as male, but he'd moved too quickly for her to see his features. Ridiculous to be afraid. Whoever it was had to be one of the camp faculty.

She took a breath. "Hello?"

He stepped forward, and the light fell over the unruly mop of thick brown hair, the aquiline nose, the square-cut jaw. Fear vanished, swept away by a burst of anger. Anger and disbelief. How could he possibly be here?

But be here Joel Brandon was. Not only that, he looked so totally at home that he might have been there for years. He wore a gray sweatshirt that had been cannibalized, leaving gaping holes where the sleeves should have been. One of them was in a tight scroll, tied as a sweatband around the dark-brown head, keeping the perspiration from streaming down that sculptured face. In his hand he held a broom; she'd caught him in the act of sweeping the floor.

A hundred questions pounded inside her head, and a heavy pulse beat in her throat. Why was he here? Mirroring equal parts dismay and relief, her eyes drifted downward. The sweatshirt was thigh length, which was a good thing. It was all he had on. At least, it looked as if it was all he had on. Below the tattered, ribbed band was that long length of bare, furred, muscled leg she'd seen that night at the club, ending in a well-shaped, equally bare foot.

Joel Brandon in the city—civilized, taut with fatigue, wallowing in females up to his knees, arrogantly expecting her to fall into his arms—had been relatively easy to walk away from. A countrified Joel Brandon, half-naked and smiling as if he'd landed a prize trout, was not going to be so easily forgotten. "How did you get here ahead of me?" she demanded.

"I flew."

He wasn't a hallucination. He walked and talked. Tonight he didn't look nearly so tired. He looked formidable. She tried again. "You flew?"

"Yes, flew." That wonderful, mobile mouth was as sober as a Sunday preacher's.

"On your broom?"

Her dry words made him grin. He brandished the genuine article and made a couple of expert sweeps.

"This is my domestic model. I parked the supersonic outside."

Her lips lifted in a rueful smile. Looking encouraged, he stepped more fully into the light. Even dressed in the unfamiliar, informal clothes, his face was as familiar to her as her own. As was his mouth. There simply was no forgetting that mouth and the way it lost its austere wariness and settled into lines of lazy male amusement. "The others thought you weren't coming tonight, but I knew you wouldn't be able to resist driving straight through so you could get organized before morning."

That little prickle lifted tiny hairs at the back of her neck. He knew her far too well. She wished she hadn't stopped outside the door; she felt silly standing there with the screen between them. "Would it be too much to ask if I could come into my own cabin?"

She couldn't see his eyes, but she knew they must be bright with the same amusement that lifted his mouth as he said with mocking suaveness, "By all means, come in and make yourself at home."

It suddenly occurred to her that walking through that door might be more dangerous than she suspected. Perhaps she ought to ask a few questions first. "What exactly are you doing here?"

His eyes wide with mock surprise, he hoisted his broom a few inches off the floor. "I'm cleaning."

"You flew to the mountains ahead of me—"

"On my broom," he added helpfully.

"On your broom," she echoed in a wry tone, "to clean my cabin." He was so determined to play it lightly, to act as if what had passed between them the night before had never happened, that she was annoyed. "Let's try this one more time. How did you get here ahead of me?"

"You stopped in Syracuse to rent a car and drive up 181. I came straight here from New York on a charter flight."

That gave her pause. He had chartered a plane to go where he knew she would be. "The bigger question is why did you come at all?"

His eyes flickered away, giving her the distinct feeling that whatever he was about to say wasn't quite the truth. "I wanted to see you. And if Muhammad won't come to the mountain, et cetera." He laid the ripped sleeve of his sweatshirt over his arm as if it were a napkin and, like a meticulous waiter escorting her to her table, came toward the door, opened it and bowed. "Would mum care to step in?"

The accent and the butler's manner were flawless. He was an accomplished mimic, this rogue male, and he was mocking her. From inside her cabin. He'd made it impossible for her to protest, impossible for her to understand what it was he was doing. He had obscured with banter his reason for being here. It was like fighting a marshmallow. There was no defense against him.

Alison thought about turning around and getting back into her car, but then she remembered her empty gas tank. Recklessly tempted to bow to the inevitable, yet afraid she would regret her impulse, she picked up her cases and stepped through the door he held open for her.

"Is there something wrong?"

"I was just wondering if the champagne is on ice." She'd have to play this silly game. Just now there didn't seem to be any alternative.

"I'm sorry, no." If he felt pleasure at her capitulation, not a trace of it showed in his face. He smoothed the rough, wrinkled edges of the sweatshirt sleeve with the contriteness of a discomfited servant caught out. "If I had known mum was arriving tonight . . ."

Memory, instant, unwanted, washed over Alison. Before, a hundred years ago, when they had first fallen in love, they'd done this kind of thing spontaneously and often, falling into roles and playing off each other as easily as children. He enjoyed silliness of all kinds, was more than willing to sustain a charade if it meant a laugh or two. It was frightening, this ability he had to summon up in her a love for foolishness that she'd almost forgotten. Very. . . frightening. Abruptly she stopped playacting. "I still don't understand how you knew where I was going and got here ahead of me."

His brown eyes flashed. "I hate to admit this, but my sister is a fink. She squealed on you. After that, it was easy. Everyone here thought you'd planned to stay overnight in a motel in Syracuse. But I had a feeling you wouldn't. That's why I was cleaning up the place tonight." Joel came a step closer, and eyes that reminded her of a tiger's, golden eyes with brown rims, gazed at her, frankly taking her measure. Accompanying the examination were the murmured words, "You should have stayed over. You look exhausted." He had a peculiar knack for delivering the most ordinary words as if they were lines in a play.

"Didn't we just act out this scene in the opposite roles twenty-four hours ago?"

"Yes, I believe we did." In the muted glow of the lamp, the bronze hollow of his throat came into view, a deep, vulnerable well of skin, surrounded by hard bones that looked as if they'd be interesting to touch.

Disturbed by her sexual attraction to him, an attraction she couldn't seem to deny, she said, "Joel, you must have had commitments, places to be, things to do. Why did you go to all this trouble?"

"Because I'm a nature lover?" he ventured, his brows lifting in droll mockery of his own words.

Her chin came up. "Nature, Mr. Brandon?"

His smile widened, and those attractive laugh lines on each side of his mouth deepened. The strength and force of her reaction seemed to give him a perverse pleasure. "Precisely, Ms Powell. So much so that I've . . . enrolled in one of your classes."

She felt as if he'd punched her in the stomach. "You can't mean that."

Tension hung in the air like fog. "Oh, but I do. I have paid my money and registered. Be nice to your future pupil, won't you?"

To give herself time to deal with the latest bomb he'd handed her, and to block out the thought that he obviously meant what he said about joining her class, she turned her head to look around her at the cabin, wondering how she could possibly stop this comic juggernaut from walking into her life and taking it over. "You aren't serious."

"It may be hard for you to believe, but yes, this time I am. And don't try to think of ways you can have me kicked out. You can't. I got the boss lady's approval."

She kept her head turned away, which had the added advantage of taking Joel out of her vision, a Joel who was just as aggressively masculine in his ragged sweatshirt as he was in every other stage of dress and undress that she'd witnessed. The cabin was clean and aired. The table shone, the kettle boiled over a gas flame on the stove…and in the corner, the bed had been made with clean sheets and a quilt.

It was an old-style bed with a high headboard of dark, gleaming walnut. Carved-wood grapes hung in clusters on each side, no doubt a long-ago craftsman's idea of a fertility symbol. The quilt looked handmade, in a wedding-ring pattern. Conscious of him watching her look at the bed, she brought her gaze back to his face and scrambled to think of some bland words that would relieve the heaviness in the atmosphere.

Her eyes bright with challenge, she said, "Do you think paying the tuition entitles you to sleep with the teacher?"

He stared at her for a moment, and then a rueful smile lifted his lips. "I wasn't that optimistic, no. But if the teacher cares to do a little after-hours tutoring—"

"The teacher doesn't."

He took the thrust of her words with no show of emotion. He said easily, taking the pressure off, "You must be thirsty after your trip. Can I get you some tea?"

Without waiting for her answer, he turned to tend the kettle bubbling on the stove.

Slippery. The man was definitely slippery. She stood watching that broad back bend as he did something at the stove, something she was sure was totally unnecessary. He had turned his back to her to give her breathing space. Along with his physical attributes, broad shoulders, muscular arms, nicely shaped legs, the man was too perceptive, too sensitive. His particular brand of challenge was as seductive as a sea breeze. She had to get him out of here.

"Isn't this a little far to go for revenge?"

He was still for a moment; then he pivoted slowly. "Revenge?" His humor had fallen away. There was something in that hard-boned face she didn't like. "What makes you think I came for revenge?"

"Why else would you come?"

The brown eyes glittered for a moment with that unfamiliar strength of purpose. "Maybe because I wanted to see you."

"I can't imagine why."

"Try harder," he said softly.

"I . . . don't want you here."

"That's unfortunate." He folded his arms and leaned against the stove. "I'm afraid we're stuck here for the night . . . together."

She searched for the amusement in his eyes, the tilt of his lips, and found neither. "What?"

"There was a little mix-up. I'm contracted to work a club up here, and I was supposed to occupy a cabin in a group that backs onto yours, owned by the same landlord. They weren't expecting me tonight, either, and my cabin was occupied, so they put me in the only other available empty one...yours. We'll have to share."

"Share? What do you mean share?"

"What share usually means. Staying here together." He paused for a moment, his dark gaze carefully unrevealing.

"That's impossible."

"Are you accusing me of lying to you?"

Those brown eyes searched her face with a seriousness that made her feel petty. She reached desperately for solid ground. "Yet another scene that we played twenty-four hours ago."

"With a few minor changes," he agreed. "Last night I asked you to live with me, with all that the term implies. Tonight I'm merely inviting you to stay under the same roof with me. There is one major difference between the two invitations—"

"I'm aware of the difference."

"Are you? A minute ago, you seemed...confused."

"Look, this has gone past the point of being funny."

His eyes roved slowly over her face. "As I said before, I save my jokes for the stage. You'd better let me fix you that tea." He paused for a moment, his eyes going over her once more, this time with elaborate innocence. "You don't think I planned this?"

She returned his look with a bland, unreadable one. "Why would I think that?"

He didn't move, as if he was thinking about it, and she was pleased to have momentarily disconcerted him.

Then he said, "Why don't you sit down and—" an eyebrow went up in amusement "—make yourself at home?"

She did need tea . . . or something. Time to think, mostly. She sank into the wooden chair, which was more comfortable than it looked, while he moved around, getting the cup and tea bag out of the cupboard, pouring hot water, putting the saucer on top of the cup to let the tea steep. He obviously knew where everything was.

"I'll find another place to stay," she said to his broad back. "I saw a motel on the way—"

"All booked up. Full of parents attending a Scout convention." His tone was easy, less intent than it had been a moment ago, when he'd asked her if she thought he was lying. She had known he had pride, but she hadn't guessed how much.

He set her teacup on the table, asked if she needed sugar. When she shook her head, he turned a chair around and straddled it, far enough back from the table so that she could see a dark edge of fabric riding his thigh just under the ribbing. Under that relic of gray cotton, he was wearing his swim trunks. She averted her eyes, only to raise them to muscular arms folded over the back of the chair, the hole where his sleeve should have been giving her a view of a lean chest covered with a smattering of dark hair. Her mouth went dry. She raised the cup to her lips, preparing herself to take a careful sip.

Taking strength from the hot, tasty liquid, she said, "Will your cabin be available tomorrow, or is this situation to continue indefinitely?"

His eyes gleamed with laughter. "I don't think so, but we won't really know until morning."

"Maybe I'd better look for another place to stay on a permanent basis."

He gazed at her, his face smooth, complacent. "The motel has been booked for the rest of the summer. My agent checked into the one lone accommodation." He was looking at her as if he enjoyed the view.

Alison's eyes shifted away, and with a casualness that she hoped was convincing, she said, "I still don't understand what made you decide to leave New York and venture into the mountainous wilds to work."

"Is your non sequitur meant to drag me away from the subject of our spending the night together?"

She gave him a straight look. "Yes."

His smile faded. "I needed a vacation to save my sanity. My agent arranged this for me."

She sipped her tea, felt it reviving her. She could almost believe him. He was in dire need of a rest; she knew that. "I can't stay here with you."

"I don't see that you have any choice."

"Oh?"

"Besides, motel hunting at night could be dangerous, even if there were more than one in the area."

"Dangerous?"

"About a month ago, a young woman who looked something like you was driving up here by the lake when—boom—she had a flat tire."

It was going to be a full-blown monologue, she knew. But whether it was a true one or one he was making up as he went along, she had no idea. "Is this going to take long? It's late, and I'm tired."

He ignored her and continued. "She didn't know how to change the tire, but she decided to give it a go."

"Well, at least she wasn't one of those helpless-female types who stand at the side of the road and wait for a man to come along."

He lifted an eyebrow and gave her a look of mock exasperation. "This story is going to take a lot longer to tell if you keep on interrupting me."

"Sorry."

"You aren't, but I'll forgive you. Now where was I?"

"You were at a decision point in the story." At his bland look, she said in a passable Cockney, "She'd just decided to give it a go, guv'nor."

He chuckled. "Oh, yes, how could I have forgotten? Well, as you said, she was a game sort, so she got the jack out and the tire iron and was jacking up the car when she heard a sound behind her. It was a strange sound, a low, feral growl. Animal. Primitive. Hungry."

Despite her skepticism and her unwillingness to get involved in the tale, the hair went up on the back of Alison's neck. As if he knew exactly what effect he was having on her, Joel paused.

After waiting the right amount of time to let her fully register the prickling of her nerves, he continued. "She gripped the tire iron and whirled around . . . and what do you think she saw?"

"Is that my cue to say 'What'?"

Dropping his dramatic story-telling voice, Joel shrugged. "If you like. It's optional. I go on telling the story, either way."

"I was afraid of that. All right, I'll bite. What did she see?"

"She saw . . . nothing."

"Nothing?"

"Nothing. So she turned back and was in the process of loosening the first lug nut . . . when she heard the sound again. That same low, savage growl. She told herself it was nothing and kept working. Then . . . something brushed her shoulder. She turned, expecting to see empty darkness . . . and there stood a big, black bear. He lumbered up on his hind legs till he was seven feet tall, and he had huge teeth and claws and eyes that glowed with evil intent."

Alison cocked an eyebrow. "And then he offered to change the tire for her."

"Oh, no. He wasn't a gentlemanly bear."

"Well, what did he do?"

Joel paused, his eyes on hers. "He had her for a midnight snack," he said matter-of-factly, "and licked his paws when he was finished. As I said, he had no manners. They found the tire iron the next day, exactly where she'd left it, locked on the lug nut, the end of it wedged in the ground. She didn't even have time to pick it up and hit the bear on the head."

She was caught in that curious place between laughter and horror. "You . . . are joking, aren't you?"

"Several witnesses saw the car. They searched for her . . . but all they found was a bit of blue scarf clinging to the branch of a tree . . . and the little fingernail of her left hand."

Unable to stop herself, Alison shuddered. "How can you sit here and tell me that horrible story? I can't believe it actually happened—"

"There was one final bit of conclusive proof." Another expertly timed pause. Alison waited, knowing instinctively that this was the punch line. "The bear showed up a few days later at the place where she worked and asked for her job." He stared at Alison, deadpan. "Unemployment is really bad around here."

She laughed then; she couldn't help it. He'd played her out as skillfully as a fisherman spinning a line for a fish. "The next bear I see, I'll tell him he can have my job, no questions asked. All he has to be able to do is corral thirty kids running loose in a park in the two seconds before the bus leaves and knock out a new set of lesson plans every week, and he's in."

"Is that what you do?" He was quietly serious, all signs of the needling storyteller gone.

"That's what I do. I'm just a teacher, Joel, and it's not a glamorous job." Not wanting to think about the difference between their lives or how pedestrian hers must sound to him, she rose to stretch her locked muscles. She went to the sink to rinse her cup and then turned to him.

"Your job is ten times more important than mine." His dark eyes took their measure of her.

"There are some days when I think the most important thing in the world is the ability to generate laughter. You have a wonderful talent, Joel. It's a great gift to be able to make people laugh."

"Alison..."

She straightened away from the stove, suddenly feeling very weary and wishing she hadn't been quite so candid with him. She felt empty, drained. "If you don't mind, I'll leave my suitcase here."

"Where are you going?"

"To sleep in my car. I have reclining seats."

Joel looked casual, but there was a tenseness about him. He'd guessed why she was closing off the conversation. "You'll be safe enough there, I guess."

"You guess?"

"I've seen bears put their paws through glass, looking for food in a car. But I'm sure they wouldn't do that to you."

It was a blatant attempt to scare her into staying in the cabin, just as the bear story had been. She wasn't going to stand around and listen to any more of his nonsense. "I'm going now. I suppose I'll . . . see you in the morning."

"I suppose you will," he murmured.

The tension sang in the room, emanating from his eyes...and her skin. She went to the door. "Good night, then."

"Good night, Alison." He sounded amused. What had she said that was funny? She went to the screen door, pulled it open and stepped onto the porch. Her footsteps echoed hollowly into the quiet darkness. The silence was palpable, thick enough to stifle her breathing, and outside it was darker than the inside of a closet.

The trees sighed in a soft movement of air that was too slight to be called a breeze. A gentle, whuffing sound reached her ears. An animal, breathing heavily. A big animal. Then she heard, more distinctly, a low growl. Cool, logical sense vanished, and primitive fears rode in on their wake. Her neck stung and so did her arms. Tiny hairs were rising everywhere in preparation for fight or flight, adrenaline pouring into her bloodstream. She knew about bears, knew that for the most part you simply stayed away from them. Telling herself her imagination was working overtime, she took a step closer to the end of the porch. The growl sounded again . . . louder and closer. She turned and bolted into the cabin.

Joel was standing with his back to the stove, exactly where he'd been when she'd left him. His expression was sober, empathetic. Something about his face made her wonder. Had he heard the sound she'd heard? If he had, he wouldn't be standing there looking so unruffled.

"Change your mind about staying?" he asked smoothly.

"No. Yes."

"So." The eyelids dropped. The mouth was controlled, unrevealing. "Shall we flip a coin to see who sleeps on the couch?"

"I'll take the couch."

"I hope you don't expect me to be a gentleman and refuse."

"I don't expect anything from you, except the directions to the bathroom."

"You didn't...hear anything out there, did you?" *Had* he heard the sound, too? Now she knew that nothing on this earth would make her venture out into the dark again, not even Joel. He moved, coming toward her with the grace of a cat. His eyes caught the light, gleamed gold. As he came closer, his bare arms brushed hers. His skin was warm, satiny with perspiration, while underneath lay that rock-hard muscle. "Would you feel safer if I locked the door?" A well-timed pause, an actor's pause, the lines around his eyes threatening to crinkle.

"Yes. Yes, I would."

He walked on past her, pushed the inside door shut and latched it. When he swiveled to face her, he looked...unconcerned. "The bathroom's through that door off the kitchen. There are towels in there and soap. If there's anything else you discover you need, you will let me know, won't you?"

He was as silky as a cat and as intelligent. Did he mean exactly what he said...or did the words carry the subtler, deeper meaning she seemed to hear in that well-modulated voice?

Alison dragged her eyes away from his tanned, hard face. "I'm sure everything is . . . in perfect order."

The wind whispered, the pines answered, and so did Joel. "I hope you find it so."

LATER, WATCHING THE PATTERN of moonlight flicker over the ceiling and trying to get her tense body to relax on the couch, Alison found she couldn't go to sleep, after all. She tried. But the bizarre evening kept going around in her mind. After coming out of the bathroom, she'd scrambled desperately to fill that waiting, intimate quiet between them by saying inconsequential things. He'd responded politely. He had said she looked tired, and he was sure she needed to rest after her long trip. He'd given her a brief tutorial on the lamp, showing her the switch under the base, and suggested she leave it on in case she needed to get up in the middle of the night. All this had been said dispassionately, without a whisper of innuendo.

While he readied himself for bed, she lay on the couch, her eyes squeezed shut. It was bad enough watching him push himself away from the stove and walk toward the bathroom door with such an easy economy of movement. She wanted no glimpses of that lithe body emerging from the sweatshirt or of the dark-brown head being freed of its sweatband.

He'd taken a shower quickly, then come out and climbed into bed. She heard the springs squeak and felt a momentary stab of envy. The couch she lay on didn't have enough resiliency to squeak. In fact, it was excruciatingly uncomfortable.

Surrounded by a quiet that seemed to weigh on her ears, she pulled the sheet Joel had provided for her under her arm and turned restlessly. She should be exhausted. She wasn't. She was keyed up, nerves singing with tension. And she knew why. Joel had come to the mountains to rest and relax, but his presence here was going to send her tension level soaring to an all-time high.

Why was he here? Revenge? That seemed much more likely, but he'd denied that motive in a way that made her believe he meant it. That left only the obvious, a spot of seduction for old times' sake. That didn't make any sense. He had every opportunity to satisfy his sexual needs in New York City. He didn't need to come chasing several hundred miles after her.

She remembered the way he'd untied her dress...the way he'd looked at her when he'd asked her to move in with him. And she wondered how long he would stay in the mountains before he got tired of his cat-and-mouse game and went back to bask in the city lights. She hoped that time would be soon. She wasn't sure she could take much more of the double onslaught of his humor...and his determination.

3

JOEL PUSHED IMPATIENTLY at the light cover, listening, waiting for the rhythm of Alison's breathing to change. Prickly, full-of-pride Alison. He knew better than to insist she use the bed. It was easier to do it his way, wait until she was asleep and then carry her here.

Just as he'd decided he would have to give up his chivalrous plan, her breathing slowed. Joel tossed back the sheet and got out of bed. He started toward her, remembered his state of undress, muttered to himself and reached for his jeans.

She lay on her side like a child, her hand curled under her cheek. Her red-gold hair surrounded her face like a golden aura. At the base of her throat, a dark hollow invited him to explore.

Bracing himself, he bent and scooped her into his arms. The contact of her sleep-warmed flesh against his night-cooled skin made him want to go on holding her in his arms until he was as warm as she was.

As if she sensed his longing, she stirred. "Hush. Everything's all right," he whispered, lying through his teeth. There were parts of his body that were decidedly not all right.

He carried her to the bed and gently deposited her in the warm nest he'd just left. She snuggled into the pillow and tucked her chin down.

He stood stock-still, ordering his body to move away from her, but there were a thousand things he wanted to do, and leaving her alone in bed was not one of them. He padded to the door, tugged it open and stood in the night coolness, breathing deeply. Looking out into the darkness, he remembered what Ted had said. "Did it ever occur to you that having money has made you damned arrogant about getting what you want?"

He put a hand out and leaned against the frame, the wood cool and damp under his palm. With his night-adjusted eyes, he could see the shadows of the trees dancing in the clearing.

Maybe Ted was right. Maybe he was getting arrogant and high-handed. Maybe he was more like his father than he thought. But, damn it, he couldn't let her walk away from him. Not this time. Not when he had everything he hadn't had three years ago.

Now the time was right. For him. Was it right for her?

She wasn't indifferent to him. She just didn't . . . like him much. How was he going to get her to like him? He jammed a hand into the pocket of his jeans. He didn't know.

ALISON FELT THE BRIGHT LIGHT, the warmth surrounding her. Forcing her heavy lids to lift, she opened her eyes and tried to make some sense of what she saw. The sun filtered through the cabin window and back-lighted the head of the man standing over her, making his hair a gold-brown halo, sheening his bare torso, obscuring his face.

"Good morning," he said.

"Good . . . morning."

"Did you sleep well?"

She came awake with stinging suddenness and realized she was no longer on the couch. She was lying in the bed, and she'd obviously been there most of the night. "I think I did." She patted the bed, looking over at the couch, where the quilt was thrown back and his pillow lay. "Did someone suspend the laws of physics while I was asleep?"

Joel, in jeans, looked washed and combed. And startled. "Good God. Do you always wake up in the morning sounding like a science teacher?"

Her eyes met his. "No one's ever complained about it before."

The quiet echoed in the cabin. Joel stared at her, wondering if she meant she hadn't had other lovers . . . or she had and they hadn't complained. The words fit either way. Did the woman always wake up armed to the teeth? "I wasn't complaining . . . exactly." His mind clicking over at warp speed, he adopted a lighter tone. "What would you like served up for you this morning, coffee, tea or . . ." He paused, another of those well-timed comedian's pauses, letting her fill in the blank, his eyes locking with hers. "Never mind the third choice. I've already discovered you're better at early-morning repartee than I am."

Smiling, Joel leaned back against the table, distancing himself from her a bit, and at this angle she could see his face.

He was a charming liar. All she could think of in reply was "Joel . . ."

For a brief moment the amusement vanished. Then, matter-of-factly, he pushed himself away from the table, said, "Right, coffee it is," and went to the stove to pour her out a cup.

She moved to swing her legs out of bed . . . and remembered her less-than-conventional nightgown. His back to her, Joel said, "Go ahead and take a shower. This will still be hot when you're finished."

A few minutes later, showered and dressed, she came out of the bathroom. A small, feminine voice wafted across the room from the outside door.

"Hello."

Saucer eyes stared back at Alison from outside the screen. A feminine urchin around three feet tall and five years old, with russet curls and stubby legs, stood with her nose pressed to the screen door.

"Hello." Alison's lips curved. Where had this charming cherub popped up from? Today was registration, but very few children came.

The child's eyes moved from Alison to Joel, where he sat at the table, his hands cupped around his coffee mug. "Are you a mommy and a daddy?"

"Now there's a blockbuster opening," Joel murmured.

"Do you have any kids?" she added.

Alison cast a quick glance at the child. When it was apparent the girl hadn't heard him, she said in an undertone, "You're the comedian. You think of an answer."

Softly, his eyes on her, he murmured to Alison, "How about 'Not that we know of'?"

Alison rolled her eyes heavenward.

"Do you?" the girl persisted from the other side of the door.

With a feeling that she'd gotten out of bed and stepped into double trouble, she said, "No, honey, we don't have any kids. Are your parents here to register you for the nature camp?"

Soberly the girl nodded. "If you're not a mommy and a daddy, how come you're having breakfast together?"

Joel, looking like the devil on a fine day, smiled. "The kid's good. I wonder if she writes her own material or contracts it out."

"Are you gonna teach us about the birds and the bees? Daddy said you would, but Mommy said no."

"Better and better," murmured Joel, turning falsely innocent eyes up to Alison. "Are you gonna?"

"'Scuse me, I gotta go. There's my mommy." The child turned and skipped off the porch.

At the stove, Joel poured out their coffee, turned and handed her one of the mugs. His eyes were dark with laughter and something more intimate. "She would leave just when it was getting interesting. Are you responsible twenty-four hours a day for dozens of cherubs like her?"

"This is a day camp. The children who come either live around here, or else their parents camp in the area for the duration of the three-week session." Fighting to ignore the appeal of those tigerish eyes, Alison took the cup from him and went to sit down at the table. "I thought you locked that door last night."

"I got up in the middle of the night and opened it. I was warm. Are you ready for breakfast? I wrestled the bakery-truck person to the ground and took some doughnuts hostage." He picked up a brown bag and shook it recklessly over a plate, making the doughnuts tumble out.

"Male or female?"

Joel picked up a doughnut and turned it over, peering at it. "I didn't ask. Is it important?"

"Not the doughnuts, the driver."

Joel laid down the doughnut with deliberate slowness, his eyes finding Alison's. "Is it important?" he repeated with soft intentness.

Alison brushed past him, heading for the stove to replenish her coffee. She was in need of caffeine stimulation if she was to continue this fencing match with Joel. "I'm sure you'll understand when I tell you I have a busy day today and I—"

"I already talked to Eve Cunningham. She asked me to tell you that she had nothing pressing and that you were to take it easy today, go for a hike or a swim, whichever appealed to you."

"I think I need a swim."

"Sounds good to me."

THE WATER WAS AS CRISP AND COOL as a mountain stream, a degree or two under sixty, just the way she liked it, good for hard swimming. After doing what she guessed was thirty laps, Alison hoisted herself up on the dock, water streaming from her neck and arms. Shivering a little, she stretched out on the beach towel she'd brought with her, turned her face to the sun, then stretched to full torsion in air already warm from the sun, preparing to enjoy the slight toasting she meant to give her skin.

She started to close her eyes and couldn't. There was too much of Joel Brandon's flesh in view. Acres of it, stretched over the taut muscle and well-sculpted bones of his legs and arms. He stood on the dock as if he owned it, his neatly turned thigh and furred chest worthy of a centerfold spread in *Playgirl*. The narrow strip of black bikini trunks was the only thing that kept him from rating a luscious X.

Something wrenched deep inside Alison, heat within her spiraling upward. He was...spectacular, smoother and sleeker and with more dark hair curling on his chest and thighs than she'd remembered.

She curled her fingers into her palms. She wasn't a fool; she knew what she was feeling. She couldn't remember having felt this strongly about him before. She couldn't remember this jolt of electricity that seemed to be coming from deep inside her.

All right, so he was dazzling. Much more so than she'd remembered. So she had a faulty memory. She hadn't expected to be sexually attracted to Joel Brandon all over again, but even if she was, she would get over it.

"Hi. Fancy meeting you here."

Funny, Alison thought, *he seems self-conscious.* "Hello, Joel."

She was wearing an electric-blue maillot cut high on the hips. It wasn't as revealing as a bikini, but it was flattering to her skin and coloring. Was he looking down at her, taking in the lightly tanned length of her leg? She didn't know. She didn't want to know.

He cleared his throat. "Guess I'll go for a swim."

"The water's a little cold, not fit for city folk. I'd give it another day or two, if I were you." She took her arm away from her face and sat up.

"You went in, didn't you?"

He looked cool enough, but his male ego was dented; she could see that. "Yes, I went in. But I'm used to swimming in cool water."

"It can't be that bad." He arched his arms over his head and dived cleanly, a graceful curve of male power plunging into the sparkling blue water.

Under the water, Joel froze with shock. It was like jumping naked into the Arctic Sea. He surfaced, tossing the water out of his eyes. The shock of the cold had him gasping for breath. His lungs contracted, and his body felt as if it were trying to turn itself inside out. He should have listened to her.

Aware he might drown if he couldn't get his breathing regulated, he turned over and began a fast crawl, churning through the water, determined to stay immersed at least long enough to salvage his pride.

How many minutes spent in this subzero bath was his pride worth? He'd never be warm again in his life. He gritted his teeth, determined to stay in the water a little longer, when he felt the cramp, a bone-racking pain siphoning up from his foot. He kicked harder, thinking the cramp would leave him. It didn't. He had to admit defeat. He circled and headed toward the dock, pulled himself up on those deceptively warm boards.

Alison was lying on her back with her arm over her eyes. Thankful she wasn't watching him shiver, he snatched up his towel and swathed his shoulders in the terry cloth, then began to massage the arch of his foot.

"Enjoy your swim?" Alison's silky voice came out from under that shapely arm draped over her forehead.

With great effort he controlled the chattering of his teeth long enough to say, "Yes, very much." He went on kneading his cramped foot, wondering if the pain would ever go away, when his towel brushed her thigh, telegraphing the fact that he was moving. "What are you doing?" She pulled her arm from her face and sat up.

With the full force of her eyes on him, he hadn't a chance of hiding the truth.

"You got a cramp, didn't you? Where?"

"Just my...foot."

She gasped with alarm and scrambled up on her knees to get closer to him, reaching under the towel for his foot. He appreciated the concern, but even more he appreciated the unobstructed view she was giving him of her throat and the sleek curves of her breasts. Deep within him, new nerves came to excruciating life. She didn't seem to notice. She was examining his foot as if she were the resident nurse, asking, "Where does it hurt? Here?"

"Underneath...." He stared down at her slender hands smoothing over the curve of his foot, wondering how it would feel to lie here in the hot sun and let those warm fingers explore his body with the heated, passionate thoroughness he knew she was capable of....

"Or here?" She probed his arch, homing in on the pain like a woman with radar in her fingers.

His flinch told Alison she'd been accurate. She grasped his foot with both hands, her teeth coming together a little because she knew she would hurt him. She had to amplify the pain before she could ease it. She concentrated on massaging his cold flesh, acutely aware that she was partially to blame for his suffering. She should have tried harder to stop him from jumping into the cold lake. She went on massaging his foot, molding the arch like pliable clay, willing the knotted muscle to relax.

Joel's cramp eased under her probing, expert massage. He was no longer in pain, at least not from his foot. He could tell her to stop anytime now...but he didn't want to. Sitting here having her touch him, even knowing he would pay for it later, gave him an acute pleasure that tightened all the nerves in the center of his body. "I didn't know water could be so cold and not be ice. Thank you. That's much better."

She didn't look up. Her hair had fallen over her shoulder, as shiny as red gold in the sun, and her face had taken on a look of earnestness. Suddenly he knew she enjoyed touching him, too, but had convinced herself she was doing it because he needed the therapy. "Relax and let me bring some blood back to your Popsicle toes."

His eyes on her face, he murmured, "Whatever you say."

As easily as if they were still lovers, she grasped his other foot and rubbed it. Under the friction of her hands, his skin warmed. He could feel the muscles in his legs relaxing...and other muscles in his body tightening. He had always enjoyed Alison's hands on his body. Always. Her skin bare and silky, her hair like fire, she looked like a golden goddess in the sunlight.

As if somehow she'd read his mind, she began to draw her hand away. He reached for her, shackling her wrist with his finger and thumb, all pretense of impersonality gone, his hold on her possessive...and sexual.

Alison's eyes flew to Joel's face. There wasn't a hint of a smile lurking in his eyes. He was simply watching her, waiting for her reaction.

She reached deep inside herself for control, struggling to look as if nothing had happened, as if her world hadn't turned upside down in the past few minutes. "I take it this means you're feeling better."

His mouth curled up in a smile. "You tell me. Do I feel better, Alison?"

He watched carefully, but there wasn't a sign of re-action from her. "Let go of me, Joel."

He hesitated for a moment, as if he planned to con-tinue holding her against her will. Then his palm slid away, dragging over the slender bones of her wrist, sending messages of acute shock along her leg. "You enjoy touching me, Alison . . . just as much as I enjoy touching you."

How soft his voice, how intent. In the silence of the warm morning, the lake lapped the dock, making slapping sounds against the supporting posts. In the si-lence she sat looking at him, and the gleam in his eyes told her he was quite willing to go on lobbing the truth over the net at her as long as she gave him the oppor-tunity.

"There were never any problems with the physical side of our relationship—you know that." She lifted her chin, squinting a little in the sunlight, her smile wry. "My mistake was in thinking that the couple who laughed together stayed together." She got to her feet . . . and so did he, lazily, with an ease that betrayed his strength.

"Was it a mistake, Alison? Or was breaking up the mistake?" He pulled the towel more tightly around her, his hands rubbing her shoulders lightly to warm her, his body at a slight angle to hers. "What do you plan to do? Spend the rest of your life looking for a square Joe who has nothing on his mind but bringing home the bacon?"

The look in his eyes and the caress of his hands brought heat surging up from the pit of her stomach.

To combat it, she turned and looked directly at him. "Life is real. Life is earnest."

The sun glittered in his eyes. "Without a laugh or two, it's damn boring."

"I'm not against a laugh or two. I just . . . like a sense of order in my life . . . something your life-style lacks. You equate order with boredom."

"I do?"

"Yes, you do." She moved slightly, asking for release from the hold he had on her shoulders. "You'd better go up to the cabin and take a hot shower, or you may get a chill."

"I have to admit this mountain air is very . . . cool." He dropped his hands, his face smooth, unreadable.

She felt infinitely better without his hands on her body—of course she did. She turned to go, wondering why she felt aching and empty, too. She should be glad they'd had this confrontation now. The sooner he went to wherever he was supposed to be, the better she'd like it.

"Well, Alison. I see you found us." Eve Cunningham stood at the edge of the dock, smiling at her.

Tall, wearing a preppy T-shirt with the required alligator, a denim skirt and a flowered hat that looked like a Katharine Hepburn reject, Eve brought Alison back from the unreal world she'd inhabited for just a moment on that dock with Joel. Pulling the towel more tightly around her shoulders, she straightened to face the woman who'd hired her to teach at the science camp.

Eve's glance flickered past Alison to Joel, lingered appreciatively for a second, then returned to Alison's face. "Gorgeous morning, isn't it?" The gleam in her eyes told Alison she wasn't talking about the weather. "Joel told me you arrived late but slept well."

"Yes."

"Good. When we start with the kids tomorrow, you'll need that reserve of energy. Take care, Joel." She swung around to leave, looking as if her mind were already on other things.

"You too, Eve."

"Nice lady," he murmured as Eve disappeared through the trees.

"You made her acquaintance very quickly."

"We speak the same language."

"You do seem to make friends easily."

"Eve and I understand each other," Joel said, unperturbed. "Anything wrong with that?"

"Hadn't you better get back to the cabin and take a shower to warm up? Then, of course, you'll have to pack."

"Yes, I will, won't I?" He reached out and drew a fingertip down her cool, wet cheek, his eyes on her face.

"Please don't . . . do that." Under the skin he brushed so lightly, her nerves quivered with reaction.

"Don't do what, Alison?" His face showed no emotion.

"Touch me as if it were your right."

He let his hand drop to his side. "Once upon a time it was."

She straightened slightly, lifting her chin. "Once upon a time belongs in stories."

"And there's no room in your world for make-believe . . . or me." His tone was light, casual. He lifted his shoulders nonchalantly, turned his back to her and walked off the dock and up the path.

She stood watching him go, hurting in some vague way that she couldn't describe. It was for the best; of course it was. He'd come to the mountains the same way he'd climbed that water tower a few years ago, on an impulse. Whatever whim had brought him here would take him away again. But standing there, watching his lithe, almost bare body disappear into the forest, she felt a sense of loss.

In a curious state of suspension, Joel walked into the cottage. The doughnuts still sat on the plate, a mute testimony to the hopes he'd had of having a breakfast conversation with Alison. The failures of the night before were there for anyone to read. The blanket he'd used on the couch was thrown over the back of it, while the bed where she'd slept was an open cocoon in the shape of her body. Separate people sleeping alone. If things had been different . . . He pulled his duffel bag from the corner where he'd tossed it and went in to take a shower.

A few minutes later, stripped of his clothes, standing under the hot water, he thought about Alison. Damn it, nothing had changed in the years they'd been apart, nothing. They'd been good friends, and making love had seemed a natural progression. The rapport he felt with her was still as strong as ever. She felt it, too; he knew she did. Had he thought she would fall into his arms last night? *Guess again, Brandon. The lady isn't interested.* But maybe . . . maybe . . . Was it his imagination, or had she softened a little while rubbing his foot? He thought she had.

Maybe the lady wasn't as indifferent as she thought she was. Having her touch him had given him pleasure, and unless he was mistaken, it had given her pleasure, too.

He stuck his face under the spray and sputtered in the water. Thoughts like that would slowly drive him crazy. How was he going to persuade her to keep seeing him? There was a deep reserve in her, a reserve he both admired and wanted to smash through.

Well, what was he going to do about her? Ignore her? Or launch a full-scale attack?

Whatever he was going to do, it had to be done from a distance. She wanted him out of the cabin, and he would gain nothing by trying to stay.

Joel turned off the water, rubbed himself down with a towel and donned jeans and a sleeveless T-shirt. The shower had washed away his torpor, made him restless and edgy. Maybe he should try to get packed and get out of here before Alison returned. No, damn it, he wasn't that kind of coward. He wasn't going to leave without saying goodbye . . . and maybe saying a few other things, too.

He began to collect his shaving things, his razor and his can of shaving cream, throwing them haphazardly into the duffel bag on the floor by his feet. A wadded pair of white undershorts went on top. He hated packing under the best of conditions, and this was not the best of conditions. He grabbed up his duffel bag and went out into the main part of the room. He tossed it on the bed with one careless heave of his arm, balled his swimsuit and towel together and added them to the jumbled contents of his bag.

Alison stood at the door, watching. She'd seen Joel pack more than once and knew he wasn't particularly organized, but that mess in his bag was bad, even for him. "Will you have a place to stay by now?"

Had he subconsciously known she was there? It seemed he had. "Yes."

"Where is it?"

He straightened, meeting her eyes. "Actually, it's quite close, just a short hike down the road from here."

Too close, Alison thought. Much too close.

He kept on with what he was doing, scooping up a pair of heavy white socks and tossing them in the bag that was fast filling up. He stood up, glanced around the cabin and began to pull the zipper shut. Feeling strangely helpless, Alison stood leaning against the door. "Joel, I—" She stopped, trying to find the right words for what it was she wanted to say. In the end she fell back on a polite phrase. "If there's anything you need—"

"Now there's an opening." His brown eyes were cool, assessing. "Has it occurred to you that you do leave yourself wide open?"

"It was a polite offer, nothing more."

"Then there is something you can do for me."

"What is it?"

"Stop making polite offers." He picked up the duffel bag and walked past her, only to stop in the door and turn. In a light tone that told her nothing of what he was feeling, he said, "Watch out for bears and wolves, won't you?" Dipping his head in a mocking salute, he turned his broad shoulders to her and went out the door.

4

ALISON HAD ALWAYS ADMIRED courage, believed every woman needed it, every day. The trouble was, believing in it and having it were two different things.

All morning she worked diligently, trying to concentrate on her first class of charming little cherubs, but even while she talked, that niggling feeling in the pit of her stomach reminded her that at one o'clock she would be facing the afternoon group, the group that included Joel Brandon. That was when she would need to summon up all the courage at her command.

A hundred times that morning she swept her perspiring palms down her denims. A hundred times she nearly lost her train of thought as she taught the class a lesson on porcupines.

Finally the session was over. She stood and watched the children bound back into the school bus like lambs let out of the barn, then turned and headed for her cabin. It was high noon in the Adirondacks and unseasonably hot. The sun shone down on her fiery red-gold head as she strode past the cafeteria toward her cabin. It was lunchtime, but she wasn't hungry; she was hot. She needed a change of clothes more than she needed food. Her jeans clung to her thighs, and her hair was too long on her neck to let a breath of air in.

Inside her quarters, it was only marginally cooler. Everything she picked up seemed to fall out of her hands. The blue scarf she'd chosen to tie back her hair had a mind of its own. It refused to be rolled into a tube. It refused to wrap neatly around her gathered curls. A hundred times she'd used this scarf to tie up her hair, but today. . .

She tossed it back onto the scarred dresser with a clipped word of disgust. All right, so she was nervous. Who wouldn't be, knowing they had to face ten sixteen-year-olds and one thirty-four-year-old? Maybe he wouldn't show up. Maybe it was all a joke.

She sifted through the eye-shadow disks, makeup jars and combs in the top drawer of her dresser, looking for a headband, and discovered she hadn't packed one. Her blouse looked as if it had been dragged through a knothole; her khaki shorts were wrinkled. It was not an auspicious beginning to the afternoon. When she saw what time it was, she gave up on her hair and ran out to the picnic bench in front of the cafeteria where she was to meet with her class. Joel sauntered through the trees, and the day veered from the merely irritating to the downright soul destroying.

She'd known the pitfalls in trying to deal with a group of kids without the benefit of four walls and a schedule, but she'd told herself she could handle them. She hadn't counted on Joel Brandon's being a member of her class. And as if he wasn't enough, there was Marty.

Alison noticed him right away. Troublemakers had that knack of standing out in the crowd. While the rest gathered around her, he slouched like a miniature movie gangster on the periphery of the group, isolating himself. But even if he hadn't set himself apart physically, he would have caught her eye. Right from the crown of his carrot head down to his high-top Nikes, he flashed like a neon light. Every move he made was filled with defiance. He even pushed up the long sleeves of his red-and-white-striped polo shirt with a hard-edged grin. He was a kid who'd grown up too fast and knew too much. And to top it all off, he was far more interested in Joel Brandon than he was in science. The rest of the group had accepted Alison's casual statement that while on vacation Joel was filling in some gaps in his education. Marty was the only one who recognized Joel and took every opportunity to be near him.

She was used to teaching teenagers who were preoccupied with their own growing pains. In Iowa, though, she knew everybody and had done so from the time they were little. She knew their parents, their cousins, their uncles, their aunts. Here she was at a disadvantage. She knew nothing about Marty Shorter apart from the fact that he obviously resented being at the camp. He looked as though it was the last place in the world he wanted to be.

Deliberately Alison treated Marty with the same friendly, no-nonsense casualness with which she treated the others. She hated to label a student a troublemaker.

She had planned to start the group off with a nature walk and a short course in tree identification. At the beginning of the trail she had them settle on their situpons, cushions the camp provided made of vinyl stuffed with newspaper. They complied, even Joel squatting to sit on the bare forest floor with scattered pine needles all around and the air smelling like heaven. There, with the sun playing through the conifers as if a mischief maker had gotten control of the spotlight, she did what she hated to do—played police officer.

"Let's talk about the rules of the trail. The first rule is we stay on it." She paused for emphasis, letting her eyes rove over the group of faces, ignoring Joel's small smile. Not one registered the same emotion as the next. There was apprehension here, boredom there, long-suffering patience here, anticipation there. Alison focused on the animated face that showed an interest in the proceedings. It belonged to a girl, a girl almost too pretty to be believed, with her pale skin, green eyes and long black hair. She looked as if she should be wearing a gilded party dress rather than a serviceable shirt and jeans. "No wandering off to explore on your own, no going into the bushes to follow birds or go to the bathroom. If anyone has to do that, please go back to the dining room and use the facilities now." Feeling more self-conscious than she had in her life, knowing that Joel, with his sense of humor, was enjoying every moment of this, she plunged on. "Every day I pick a leader and that leader leads. Everyone follows in order. No pushing, shoving, hitting or kicking to get ahead in line. When we stop at a point of interest, I expect everyone to gather around and listen up. Does everyone understand the rules? Good. Let's get going. Kathryn, you lead the way."

Alison turned to find the dappled light playing over Joel's face. Suddenly he looked serious, his eyes on the freckled face of the boy next to him. In the forest primeval, Marty's immature face had taken on a dark, saturnine look. Alison felt herself reacting in a way she hadn't done since her first year of teaching, with a jolt of apprehension that tightened her stomach. This boy was pulling hidden strings in her, and she was experienced enough to know she couldn't allow that to happen.

She started along the trail. One by one they straggled after her. At a scrubby hornbeam she stopped, said its name and told those several sets of eyes turned on her that the tree was of no commercial use, that its only real value was as shelter for small animals.

"That's a funny name, cornbeam," Marty announced.

"Hornbeam," she corrected automatically. Marty's grin told her she had fallen neatly into the trap. One of the other boys giggled.

That set the tone for the whole walk. Everything was a big joke from then on. Halfway along the trail, just as Alison was about to turn back and finish her lecture in the protective confines of the lodge, Joel fell into step beside her. "Does it bother you that they're making jokes?"

"The educational value of the hike has dropped off sharply."

"Not necessarily. Research shows that people remember things better if an emotional jolt is delivered with the information, like laughter or tears." Joel's eyes met Alison's, giving her the feeling that his message carried a subtle undercurrent that she'd be better off to ignore. Her own eyes guarded, she countered, "Only if the emotion and the information are related in some way."

"Humor adds to our intelligence. It gives us a new way to see things, a way to turn words and ideas sideways, upside down, inside out. Z.Z. Topp could just as well be A.A. Bottom." She was not in the mood to encourage him and so didn't answer. They walked in silence for a moment, and then he said, "What do you have against humor, Alison?"

"Are we still talking about my class?"

"As far as I know."

"I have nothing against humor. In the proper place and the proper time, it's a catharsis—"

"You make it sound like a laxative."

She turned on him, disturbed in a way she didn't understand. In a low, furious tone, she said, "That's exactly what I mean. I try to explain how I see something and you make a joke out of it."

He stood staring back at her, looking lazily relaxed, but there was a glint of purposeful determination in his eyes that didn't match the smile on his lips. "Maybe I'm just trying to get you to stop taking yourself so seriously."

"And what happens then, Joel?" Standing behind the group of students, she pitched her voice low so that her words would be heard only by him. "What happens when I stop taking myself seriously? Do I fall back into bed with you?"

His shadowed face told her nothing. He said slowly, lazily, "Why do you view that as a fate worse than death?"

Whatever she might have replied was lost in the sound of splashing. Her teacher-protective instincts screaming like a fire alarm, Alison whirled away from Joel to scan the lake. Marty was there, wading into the water, pushing ahead of him an old canoe that had been stripped of its outer skin and obviously abandoned on shore.

Alison cried out to him to stop. Marty ignored her and, with a vigorous shove, pushed the canoe into the water, scrambled over the side and leaned forward to use his arm as a paddle to propel the boat away from shore.

She took off after him, crashing through the underbrush, aware that Joel was beside her, running as fast as she.

At the shoreline, just as she was ready to take a breath and make a shallow surface dive, Joel caught her arm.

"Let him go. With a little luck, maybe he'll drown."

The words were barely out of his mouth when the canoe began to gurgle like a fountain. The end where Mary was sitting tilted and went down. Marty let out a yell that could be heard clear over to Bear Mountain. Still Joel held Alison's arm. "Let him swim. The dunking will cool him off."

Marty's defiance turned into frenzy. Out of the jumble of words, Alison caught two: "Can't swim."

Panic flared up, full-blown. She twisted out of Joel's hand, kicked off her sneakers, took a breath and hit the shallow water flat with a gliding stroke that sent her halfway to the boat. A splash told her Joel had entered the water an instant after her.

Joel surged ahead of her and reached the boy first. He plucked him out of the water by his shirt collar. Panicked, Marty wrapped his arms around Joel's neck in a stranglehold and pushed him under. Afraid for Joel as much as for Marty, Alison cried out and swam to the tangle of threshing arms and legs. She yanked one of Marty's arms away from Joel's neck. Choking and coughing, the boy transferred his death grip to her. Then she, too, went under. She heard Joel's curse, heard him call her name. Swimming furiously, she kicked her legs down to tread water . . . and winced as her foot hit bottom. With Marty's arms still fastened around her, she got her feet beneath her and heaved herself upright.

Joel must have found footing just as she did. Water splashed in rainbow droplets as he brought Marty's head up, yelled at him to stand up and jerked his arm from around Alison's neck.

As suddenly as it began, it was over. All three of them stood in the chest-high water and stared at one another.

Even with his sweatshirt soaked and clinging to his chest, and his hair in brown silky strands plastered to his forehead, Joel looked good. Alison was sure she hadn't fared as well. Her too-big blouse was plastered to her like a second skin. Marty resembled a soaked cat, a woebegone, thoroughly wet, water-hating cat.

Her eyes met Joel's. He glanced at Marty and looked supremely satisfied at the damage the water had wrought on the young troublemaker. "Had enough of the briny deep for one day, Captain Hornblower?" He cocked an eyebrow at Alison. "What do you think, matey? Would you say the chap hasn't collected his sea legs yet?" Alison shook her head, too relieved that Marty was safe to answer. Alison's reaction brought a frown to Joel's brow. He clasped Marty's arm and escorted him to shore, his scorn for the boy palpable. On dry land he said, "The next time you try a dumb stunt like that, I'll let you drown."

"How was I to know that old tub wouldn't float?"

"You're right, there was no way you could know. Anyone with half a brain would know better than to take an old cast-off boat out onto the lake, but you don't have half, do you?"

The boy flushed under Joel's cutting words. "Big man. Big deal. You can't be too smart yourself, or you wouldn't be in a class with a bunch of dumb kids."

"Got a nickel?" Joel asked easily. When Marty nodded, Joel said, "Give it to me."

"Why should I?" Marty looked torn between curiosity and the need to look cool.

"Do it and find out why."

Marty stood still, the two conflicting urges evident on his face. In a sudden, quick movement, he thrust his hand in his soaked pocket and drew out the coin. His face mutinous, as if he was unhappy at his capitulation, he slapped it in Joel's outstretched palm. "Now what?"

"I'm going to give you a piece of advice, and I knew you'd value it more if you had to pay for it." Marty scowled. Joel ignored his dark face and went on in the same easy, relaxed tone. "The spoken word is a two-edged sword. It cuts both ways. You use it to whack away at other people, and they'll grab it out of your hand and impale you with it. Remember that." Smiling that maddening smile, Joel turned and murmured a terse sentence to Alison. A moment later, whistling, flipping the nickel in the air with his thumb and forefinger, Joel walked away.

THAT EVENING, when the sun had turned the world mellow and the birds were quiet in the pines, Alison picked her way through the pine-needle-laden ground to see Eve Cunningham.

Eve's cabin was cool and comfortable with old knotty-pine furniture. "It matches me," Eve said dryly, pouring a generous portion of rosé wine into a grayish-brown mug that looked as if it had been made by prehistoric Indians. She poked the mug at Alison, nodding her head toward the battered cup, her mouth lifting. "Everything up here matches me. Antediluvian. That's why I feel so at home. Drink up. I never indulge in my vices alone." Those wise green eyes flicked sideways in an invitation to laugh, and another wrinkle cracked along the side of her mouth. Eve's face had the look of a woman who worshiped the sun instead of smooth skin. Perhaps that was why Alison liked her. She had her own brand of courage. It shone from those green eyes. Alison grinned back, thinking that this was the first time since Joel had walked away that afternoon that she'd felt like smiling.

"Classes go okay?" Eve was the picture of casualness, settling into the tartan cushion of the huge couch, one knee thrown over the other, her own mug of wine clasped by fingers that had a surprising delicacy compared to her no-nonsense, slightly overweight, fiftyish body. She was wearing a pair of white slacks cropped midcalf. A floppy shirt in a garish combination of blue, green and purple swirls accented her breasts and hid a multitude of sins below the waist. Her graying hair framing her face, she looked like a cross between Mrs. Santa Claus and a hip fairy godmother. Seated opposite Eve in a chair that was swallowing her at five times the rate that the ocean was rising, Alison sipped her wine.

"Or did you come to tell me about Marty?" Eve sipped and smiled, her question cloaked in easy friendliness.

"I'm not sure whether I came for confession or commiseration."

"A little of both, probably." Eve had the look of a woman who had seen too much of life to let any part of it shock her. "I've already heard a couple of Technicolor versions of this afternoon's event. Why don't you tell me yours?"

"You may not like mine any better than you liked the others."

"I didn't say I didn't like the others. Actually I was rather disappointed I wasn't there to enjoy the sight of Marty doused in the lake."

Alison wriggled in her chair, not exactly sure of Eve's reception. She seemed amiable enough, but . . . No, it wasn't Eve's reaction she was worried about; it was her own guilty conscience. She shouldn't have let any of it happen. And it wouldn't have if she'd been paying attention to her class instead of jousting with Joel. His voice, his beautiful, expressive voice when he'd asked her if going to bed with him would be a fate worse than death, had held a wealth of crisp, straight-backed pride. "Problems with Marty started before that, actually. I was pointing out the different types of trees, and I started with the hornbeam. He thought I said cornbeam." Alison smiled ruefully. "That set the tone for the whole walk. Everything was a big joke from then on."

Again Eve sent that curious little probing gaze Alison's way. "And that wasn't your idea of a well-run class, even though they were making a contribution." Eve's smile held the wisdom of her ancient namesake.

Alison rested the mug carefully on the wooden arm of her chair, thinking she really didn't need another lecture on how useful humor was in education. Eve's face was flushed with the wine and the warmth of the summer night. And the zeal of a reformer. How much of what she was saying had to do with Joel? How quickly had she fallen under Joel's spell? What was it he did to people to win them over so thoroughly? Alison felt that familiar sensation, a quick, gnawing rise of jealousy that was unwanted, unwarranted and unworthy of her. She had no claim on Joel.

Eve wasn't content to let her sit in silence. She drawled, "And were Marty and Ted the only ones cracking jokes? How about that elderly pupil of yours? I told him he had to behave himself or I'd expel him from class."

"His behavior was exemplary." She told Eve what Marty had done and how both Joel and she had rescued him. Except for the last part of the story. She couldn't share that with Eve. But for two hours she'd been remembering how Joel had turned to her slowly, squinting against the sun, and said in a soft tone that was meant for her ears alone, "Life is real. Life is earnest. See if you can keep the kid and yourself alive to see another day." He'd left her stinging from that cool, unexpected lash of his tongue.

She'd come to Eve mainly to escape that voice. And that other voice, the small echo inside her head that said he wasn't the uncaring man she had thought he was. He'd been worried about Marty, worried about her. He hadn't cracked a joke. He'd reminded her of her responsibility. Had she been wrong about Joel?

It was that unsettling thought that had driven her out of the cabin she'd shared with him for one brief night and into Eve's. Now, unable to look into the other woman's kind, nonjudgmental face, Alison's eyes dropped. "The boy might have drowned."

"I don't think so. Whatever else Marty is, he isn't suicidal. He has the survival instinct of a cat. Remember that the next time you're tempted to feel sorry for him."

Eve paused, her eyes going over the young woman. "Was it Marty's defiant runaway act that bothered you . . . or Joel's rescuing him?"

Alison raised her chin and gave the older woman a clear-eyed look. "I want to know about Marty."

Eve toyed with her mug, her face thoughtful. "If I tell you his story, will you promise me you won't feel sorry for him? I had a young woman up here last year who did that, and Marty ate her alive."

"After what he did today, sorry is not what I'm feeling for him."

Eve smiled. "All right, then. Marty isn't any different from many other kids in this country. When he was twelve, his parents were divorced and his mother remarried. The change in his household came at a bad time for him. He couldn't accept it. To complicate things, his best friend was killed in a plane crash. He's been angry at the world ever since." Eve's shoulders lifted. "His mother has tried to buy the world back for him, but he doesn't want it. He's far too intelligent for his own good. And talented."

"Talented?"

"He sings, dances, acts—you name it. That's another bone of contention between him and his mother. He inherited his ability to dance from his father, and this hasn't made her happy. His mother wants him to be a research scientist; he wants to go into the theater."

"I see."

"Do you?" Eve sighed. "Every year his mother sends him up here thinking we can accomplish what she can't, remake her son into her image. And every year Marty does his darnedest to show her there's no hope. Meanwhile, he's become a permanent fixture at the camp. The season isn't officially open till we've had our first escapade by Marty."

Alison's mouth curved in a smile. "I don't remember him being listed in that glossy brochure you sent me."

Eve flashed another of those half-wise, half-devilish smiles of hers. "I'm smarter than that."

Alison looked down into her wine mug, her mouth turned up in a rueful smile. "And I thought it would be so much fun to teach science to kids in a place where they could see it happening."

"That's why I hired you."

"I can't always depend on Joel Brandon being around when I have trouble with Marty. Do you have any words of wisdom for me about how to handle him?"

Eve's eyes gleamed with mischievous amusement. "Joel? Or Marty?"

"Marty, of course."

"Of course. Well, frankly, my dear, I thought I'd leave it to your good judgment. You've been a teacher long enough to know that if I suggested an approach, it would work for me, but it might not work for you. You'll have to plan your own strategy. Think of it as an interesting experiment. You have my permission to do whatever you think necessary, short of taking him out on the lake again and drowning him. No, don't look at me like that. Believe me, you'll want that satisfaction before the summer is over." Eve winked. "Cheers," she said, lifting her mug and downing the contents.

Easy for you to say. Watching her, Alison had the distinct feeling that Eve Cunningham was looking forward to the next six weeks with relish.

"HEY! WHAT THE DEVIL do you think you're doing here?" Joel caught the arm of the redheaded kid who lounged in the shadows of the doorway and trundled him toward the entrance of the dining room next door. The minimum age for admittance to the Pine Tree Lounge was twenty-one, and Joel knew the kid he'd fished from the water that afternoon wasn't even close. The bar was a favorite spot, set back off the road in the country among the pine trees, hence the name. Filled with an assortment of country-folk regulars plus several summer people who had grown tired of the rustic camping life and sought the closest thing to bright lights and entertainment, it was a popular, prosperous place with a friendly atmosphere. State campsites abounded around the lake areas in the Adirondacks, and the people from the campsites made up a large portion of Clay Stockton's business. Once they'd camped, they often returned the next year and stayed the two-week limit. This created a core of people who knew one another and enjoyed the yearly catch-up gatherings. In the past few evenings that he'd been there, Joel had already gotten acquainted with several couples.

Aware of a few heads turning his way, Joel mumbled a word under his breath and hoped no one would accuse him of child abuse. He thought of some choice forms for this specimen, particularly the one that involved turning the kid bottom up over his knee and placing a few well-aimed blows on that skinny rear end.

"Hey." The kid's loud-voice protest brought them more attention. "You're mussing the suit, man." He made an elaborate pretense of pulling his T-shirt away from Joel's hard fingers.

"I'll muss more than the suit if you don't come along quietly."

"I don't want to come along quietly. I came to hear Joel Brandon, the world-famous comedian. I thought you were working here. Instead you're at the bar downing a beer and bouncing innocent kids in your spare time—"

"In *their* spare time innocent kids don't frequent bars. Where in the hell are your parents?"

The boy grinned. "Got it in one, smart man." He turned back, and in the hush of the room, he said, "Hey. Tell the chick singer she's flat. In more ways than one."

Joel's grip on the boy's arm tightened. Enjoying it more than he should have, he hauled the youth through the swinging doors and over the threshold into the dining room. Heads turned, but Joel was too angry to care. "You know what you are, kid? You're one big cliché."

"Big man, big deal. Sure I'm a cliché to you. You don't even know my name."

That brought Joel's brown eyes to the boy's face. In a way, the kid was right. He hadn't cared who he was. He'd only known the youth was endangering people he cared about. Irritated at the perception behind those tight, deliberately antagonizing words, Joel tossed the boy's insolence back at him. "Why should I ask the name of a creep who, in his spare time, endangers a teacher whose only crime was trying to drive some knowledge into his thick skull, puts the honest man who runs this bar in jeopardy and insults a young woman who's doing the owner a favor by singing a few songs for the customers?"

The kid gave him a cocky grin. "I don't do too bad for a beginner, do I?"

Joel favored him with a long, considering look. "I should have let you drown."

The boy wrenched his thin arm from Joel's grasp. "Then why didn't you? Never mind, I know why. Because you couldn't resist acting the big hero for your chick."

Joel stared at the boy, wondering how any kid could be such a combination of perception and thoughtlessness. That curious mixture was familiar. Too familiar. It could have been himself standing there at sixteen. Memories washed through him, memories of days and nights spent actively seeking adult antagonism. He was hit with a sudden, gut-wrenching stab of empathy. "How did you get here?"

As if the youngster sensed Joel's softening mood, his own aggression heightened. "I hitchhiked. Any objections?"

"None that I could voice in the time we have at our disposal. Where are your parents?"

"I already told you where they were. Or you told me."

"Can it and answer the question."

The boy stared at Joel. "They went to a movie."

"So you took a hike."

A closed, blank look shuttered the boy's eyes. "They'll never know the difference."

"Where do you live?"

Joel could see the boy think about lying and then discard the idea with the arrogant decision that it wasn't worth the effort. "In Elmira. But right now the entire family is playing cozy campers at a trailer on a campsite on Fish Creek."

Joel could imagine how cozy it was with Elmira's version of James Dean in residence. He felt a fleeting sympathy for the parents, despite the fact that their carelessness had landed him with the kid. "So they left you alone. Maybe, even at your age, you don't like to be alone."

Marty's eyes went hot with resentment at Joel's perceptive comment. Tiring of the game, Joel said, "Come on. I'll take you back to the campsite."

"Don't bother. I can go back the same way I came."

"Not while I have something to say about it." Joel's jaw developed a hard slant. The boy was silent for a moment. Joel, taking advantage of this sudden compliance, took hold of his arm again and marched him forward.

"Let go of me, or I'll sue you."

Joel tightened his grip. "If you do, you'd better make sure you get a darn good lawyer." Even as the words came out of his mouth, he wondered at his own persistence. The kid had hitchhiked here; he should let him find his way back. Yet he couldn't. For if he did, in some obscure way he'd be letting Alison down. His mind told him that made no sense at all, but he wasn't in the mood to listen to whispers of caution.

5

JOEL MADE IT through the dining room, but in the entryway, in the glassed-in cubicle that acted as a windbreak between the inner and outer doors, Marty came to a halt and shot Joel a straight, adult look. "You can't take time to baby-sit me. Aren't you due to go on soon?"

Marty's rare excursion into thinking about someone else caught Joel by surprise. "My schedule's flexible. Come on. My car's off to the side."

The cool night air was like balm to Joel's face. He released the boy's arm, and silently the two of them strode across the parking lot.

Inside the car Joel started the motor, automatically drew his seat belt over him, clicking it closed, then looked over at the slightly less mutinous face of his companion. "Fasten your seat belt."

Marty gave him a sardonic look. "Aren't you stepping out of your role a little too far? Skip the concerned-father bit. Stick to being a comedian."

Joel's mouth tightened. "I'll play my part any way I choose . . . but right now, you're playing your part the way I tell you to."

"I don't wear seat belts."

Yes, there were echoes of Joel's past in Marty's voice. *Rules are for fools. I'm too smart to . . .* "In my car you do. Hurry up, get it on. Or do you want me to help you?"

His youthful companion sat silent, glaring back at him in the darkness. "You're a pain in the—"

"I am that. I'm also the one with the driver's license. Now get that belt buckled." Lord, he was tired of this kid's childishness. He had a very strong urge to turn this smart-mouthed boy over his knee.

Either his words or the tone of his voice had betrayed his impatience. His mouth twisted in resentment, Marty did as he was told. Feeling a satisfaction out of all proportion to the size of his victory, Joel stifled a small smile and threw his arm across the back of the passenger seat while he reversed out of the parking space.

On the winding highway that led to Fish Creek, a black hole of a road with the shadows of pines lined up on the side like a million sentries, Joel let the silence in the car build. Out in the cool night air, he'd breathed in a large dose of common sense. He told himself he wasn't interested in whatever thoughts were going through the kid's mind, that he didn't want to get involved. During the day Marty was Alison's problem; at night he was his parents' problem. Joel wasn't qualified for the role of Good Samaritan. He was meddling enough just taking the kid home.

Marty squirmed restlessly in his seat. The silence was evidently bothering him. "Turn on the radio, will you?"

"No," said Joel.

As if he were in shock, Marty subsided into silence. Hadn't anyone ever told him no before?

"For a stand-up comedian, you don't have much small talk." When Joel didn't reply, Marty turned his head and stared out the windshield. "You gotta have small talk, man, or you don't make it with the chicks these days."

Joel's first instinct was to go on giving this pain in the neck the silent treatment he deserved. Then, despite himself, he responded. "Aren't you a little young to be worrying about 'making it' with 'chicks'?"

"Naw. I get around."

Bravado. Sheer bravado. At least, Joel hoped it was. "Did it ever occur to you that it might be a step in the right direction to treat the 'chicks' like human beings?"

"Is that what *you* do?" There was a well-timed pause while Joel gritted his teeth, thinking maybe the kid had a point. Marty was too smart for his own good. "How's your love life these days? You making it with the teach?"

Joel twisted the wheel of the car and turned into the entrance of Fish Creek State Park, thinking it hadn't come a minute too soon. Was this what Alison dealt with every day of the school year, kids who were rude and self-centered and rapier quick with personal comments? He'd always respected her choice of career and admired her for her dedication, but never so much as at that moment.

"I'm returning this boy to his family's campsite," Joel explained to the ranger who stepped forward to check the unfamiliar car.

"You're not staying the night?"

Joel shook his head, controlling a decided tendency to shudder. The woman asked, "What number?"

Joel turned to the boy. "What number, ace?"

For a moment Joel thought he wasn't going to answer. At last he said, "Thirty-four."

"Turn right and follow the road."

"Thank you." Joel nodded to the woman, grateful she wasn't more curious about the rebellious young male specimen lounging in the passenger seat.

The only light on in the campsite was a small kerosene lantern placed on the ground a few feet away from the travel trailer. It flickered in the summer night and cast a small, radiant circle that did little to dispel the shadows around the trailer. Joel remembered the kitchen light that had been left on in an empty apartment for him, and how he'd hated that inadequate light for creating more shadows than it banished.

On the other side of the kerosene lantern, the glimmer of water shone in the darkness. Most of the campsites on Fish Creek were next to the water. The parents had gone and left a kid, one who couldn't swim, alone at a campsite near water. He was old enough to stay away from the water, but still . . .

Something deep and wrenching twisted inside Joel. He shifted in the car seat, his eyes going over the boy. "Have you got a key to the trailer?"

"Sure." He pulled a chain from the inside of his shirt. "The badge of honor. This was given in token of their trust in me and their faith in my honesty."

"Misplaced though it may be."

The boy sat staring at him. In the dim light Joel could see nothing but the cynical twist of his lips. "They've got nothing to complain about. I'm always here when they come home."

"Don't make tonight an exception."

"Why? Because you brought me home and now you feel responsible for me? Don't bother. It's a waste of your time . . . and mine."

He looked like a waif, a spitting, arch-backed kitten who'd been dumped by the wayside a week ago and hadn't eaten since. Echoes from the past washed over Joel in disturbing waves. His mouth tightening, he sat unmoving.

"Hey, funny man. You never answered my question about your love life."

Joel cast his eyes over Marty's placid face. "No, I didn't, because you never asked it. Now if you're finished with your obnoxious act, get out of the car."

In the silence the boy sat staring at Joel. Then he tipped his chin at a belligerent angle. "It's no act. This is the real me you're seeing."

"Good night, Marty." Joel's voice was soft, lethal.

"Can't wait to get rid of me, can you?" His shoulders braced, Marty turned and opened the car door. When he'd climbed out, he slammed the door shut and leaned forward, gripping the edge of the window well with his curled fingers. "Well, it looks like this is goodbye. Thanks for the ride. Sorry I didn't get to hear your routine tonight. I've seen you on TV. You're not too bad."

"Thanks. I think." Had Marty seen him looking at the campsite and its lone light? Had he been purposely rude to curb any tendency Joel had toward pity? Joel knew when he was sixteen, that that would have been his own reaction exactly. Acting on impulse, Joel thrust his hands into his pocket. The rustle of paper told him the unopened bag of peanuts in the shell was still there. He brought out the package and handed it to the boy. "Here, take these."

Round, dark eyes stared at Joel, their expression hidden by the shadows that surrounded them. "Why should I?"

"Eat them in bed and leave the shells on the floor. If anybody tries to get near you, you can hear the shells breaking. As a burglar alarm, it's cheap and effective. That's what I used to do when I was alone at night."

Marty stared at the bag and then lifted his eyes to Joel as if not quite able to believe somebody shared his fears. In the echoing silence, a camp fire from an adjacent campsite popped; a woman laughed.

"And you still carry them?"

"Sure," Joel said easily. "Contrary to what you think, I do a lot of one-nighters. It's a schedule that doesn't leave much time for 'chicks'... which means I end up spending a lot of those nights alone in strange motels in various cities throughout the country. It's a little scary."

Marty's eyes closed briefly as if he was affected by an emotion he couldn't allow the man to see. Joel's casual admission of his own fears moved Marty deeply. When he opened his eyes he said, "Then maybe I'd better give back half of them."

"No. Not tonight. I won't need them. Take it easy, kid." Still looking stunned, Marty stepped away from the car, and Joel put the car in gear. Headlights flashed over the boy as Joel turned and drove away. The scrawny redhead was still standing there, his sneakers untied, his hand holding the bag Joel had given him.

AT THE BEGINNING of Alison's class the next day, a heavy heat hung in the air, the moist thickness of the lull before a summer storm. Like the atmosphere, Marty was unnaturally constrained, an energy force denied an outlet. His reticence bothered her almost as much as his antics had the day before. His covert glances at Joel were just as disturbing as his silence. Had something happened between them? Gathering the teenagers around her and getting ready to teach, she felt she was sitting next to a volcano, waiting for the eruption, only worse, since she couldn't actually measure the seismic tremors inside Marty. She pushed her damp hair off her neck and struggled to put the boy out of her mind.

Walking through the trees with her students gave her some marginal relief from the heat and her own tension. In the shadow of the pines, the whispering calm soothed her agitation. An added balm to her soul was discovering how well her students remembered yesterday's lessons. When she began giving the verbal quiz she'd prepared, she knew that she'd been wrong about their retention. While the group stood in the sheltering trees, a safe distance away from the lake, Kathryn repeated the definition of an ecosystem: plants, animals and their nonliving environment.

"Fine," Alison said, "but what does that mean precisely?"

Without hesitation the pretty girl replied, "It means everything is related to each other and to its environment and that we, as the species of man, have an obligation to protect our wildlife and our plant life for our sake as well as theirs."

Was it Alison's imagination, or was that a faint smile lifting Joel's lips as he slouched against a tree to her right, watching? Alison said, "Excellent. Who can tell me something about the black-cherry tree?"

A gangly youth named Tom volunteered the information that the black-cherry provided furniture for man, fruit for birds and nectar for bees. A girl named Jennifer answered Alison's next question about the white oak, saying it was one of the most important tree species for wildlife because its sweet acorns were eaten by birds and animals. Unbidden, the lines of an old folk song popped into Alison's mind:

I thought my love was a sturdy oak,
but put to the test he bent and broke,
and left me weeping like the willow tree,
growing on the bank of the old Miss—er-ee.

She'd known from the very beginning Joel wasn't a sturdy oak. She'd known he had a talent for living in the moment. He had enlarged and enriched her life as no other man ever had. Yet he . . .

When had it gotten so quiet? When had ten pair of eyes all turned in her direction? She scrambled to bring her thoughts back to her class. "Thank you, Jennifer.

Now shall we talk about the part trees play in creating the earth's topsoil?''

There was no relief from the heat or the feeling of tension during the next three days, even though Joel and Marty were both quiet during class. Too quiet. Alison was at least able to draw Marty out with questions. Joel was another matter. He volunteered nothing, and though she'd been tempted to ask him a question and had looked at him once, ready to challenge him, she'd closed her mouth again. The warning gleam in those lazy brown eyes had been too vivid. At the end of the class Joel had walked away without a backward glance, the victor.

The days of the next week fell into a pattern, albeit a disturbing one. The weather stayed rich and warm, with a heaviness that left her heated and restless in her bed at night. She spent her evenings alone, filling the time until she went to bed by planning her sessions for the next day. When the tenor of her thoughts was too much for her to tolerate, she shared an occasional mug of wine with Eve.

ON THE SECOND FRIDAY NIGHT, as she sat cross-legged on the floor of her cabin, going over her plans for the next week's classes, she found her mildly annoyed state of mind escalating to downright irritation. All right, so Joel wasn't in her class to be treated like a student. It seemed he hadn't come to the mountains to pursue her, either. Then why had he gone to so much trouble to put himself in her realm? It made no sense at all. She knew where he was staying; she'd walked by the cabin that was his cozy retreat nearly every day in her nature walks with her classes. She knew where he was spending his evenings. Eve had told her he was appearing at the Pine Tree Lounge and invited her to go along and see him. Alison had refused, saying she'd caught his act in New York. Eve had arched an eyebrow and smiled.

Thinking about Joel was not helping her prepare her lesson on loons. Maybe it wasn't possible to think about working on a Friday night. She did have the rest of the weekend to plan. There were letters she could write instead. She'd received one from Tracy and owed her an answer. Joel's sister was as curious as a cat about what was going on in the mountains, and it was unfair of Alison to let her sit in New York and simmer, but she simply hadn't felt like writing. How could you write to a friend whose brother was making you feel as if you were sitting on a powder keg?

Joel. Everything came back to him. He was the reason she was sitting here going over her lesson plans as if Einstein were attending her classes. He was the reason she felt hot, restless, unsettled, closed in.... Alison tossed a pencil down on the notebook and muttered, "Damn." Why wasn't he doing something?

What is it you want him to do?

Alison got up and began to prepare for bed, washing her face with unnecessary vigor and cleaning her teeth as if Smokey the Bear had taken up dentistry and was watching her. She crawled into bed and tried to close her mind to Joel. But despite her efforts to forget him, he wreathed through her mind like curling smoke. The way he'd looked that day, clad in jeans and leaning against a tree, his face newly bronzed, his eyes dark and considering, his lean fingers on his thigh, played around her head like a picture on a revolving wheel.

He was slowly, methodically and—unless she was very much mistaken—deliberately driving her crazy.

The weekend dragged by endlessly. The thunderstorm that should have come days before broke at last, darkening the skies. Thunder racketed in the mountains, the sound and fury matching her mood. She spent a restless Saturday afternoon in her cabin, cleaning her bureau drawers, giving herself a manicure and a pedicure, listening to the rain patter on the roof and deciding that whoever thought rain was romantic needed psychiatric help. She showered, washed her hair and decided that if it rained any longer, she would make the *Guinness Book of World Records* for being the cleanest woman residing on the Adirondack mountain range. In her robe, she picked up a book by Isaac Asimov that she'd brought with her to read, thinking there might be something in it she would want to include in her teaching.

By Sunday evening, when the sky finally cleared and the temperature warmed up again, she slipped into her swimsuit and ran down to the lake. As she dived into the cold water, shock sizzled through her like lightning, but she surfaced and began to swim, determined to stay in the water. She needed the outlet of physical exercise.

Half an hour of steady swimming in the chilled water began to work its magic. Her mind nearly as numb as her body, she crawled onto the dock and wrapped herself in her voluminous towel.

The twilight enclosed her, softened the edges of the dock, turned the trees into a dark veil. The darkness at the crest of the hill shifted, changed, took on form, became Joel. Light-colored chinos clung to his thighs. A knit shirt covered his muscular chest but revealed the toned body underneath. He was essential male, dressed in the garments of civilized man, yet his very masculinity hinted at a primitive sexuality. Around her, the forest whispered ancient, untold secrets and poured rain-cleansed air over her cheeks.

At the edge of the dock, Joel stopped. Heavy lashes hid the expression in the golden-brown depths of his eyes.

The night was filled with the peep of frogs, the rustle of the trees, and yet it was quiet, too quiet. She had to say something, anything, to fill the void. "Were you . . . looking for me?"

"Yes."

The coolness in his voice intensified the quiet that followed. She clutched the towel more tightly, seeking warmth. Why, after all these days, was he seeking her out? Her mind mocked her, telling her the answer. He was an actor, a comedian. He knew the value of a timed pause. "Was there something you wanted to say to me?"

"Yes."

A fish leaped, a flash of silver in the soft light, the slap to water as it came down again resounding in the quiet. Joel remained silent. She could hear the beat of her heart, the scree of a seagull. "What . . . is it?"

"Has anything changed between us, Alison?"

Her heart cried out the answer. Nothing had changed. She loved him, but he didn't love her. She lifted her head, the cool breeze drying the moisture on her neck. "No."

"So I'm wasting my time up here." He thrust his hands into his pants' pockets. The gesture filled her with regret, loss and a simmering anger. Success-oriented Joel Brandon thought of her in terms of time wasted. "So it would seem. You'd be much better off seeking your sexual pleasures back in the city with all those women you have panting for you on your recording machine. Now if you'll excuse me, I'm getting chilled. I need to go and change."

In that soft, gray light, he stood between her and dry land, unmoving, his face a dark mask.

To Joel, those crisp, cutting words were the first hopeful sign he'd had. Then he got another; she took a step toward him. Acting instinctively, he moved onto the dock and squarely into her path.

The dock joggled with his weight and shuddered under Alison's bare feet. He was inches away, a silent barrier.

"Joel . . ." She didn't know what she'd been about to say, but it didn't matter, for the words died in her throat. He reached out and caught the edges of the towel above her breasts, using it to draw her close to him.

"You're giving me conflicting signals, sweet. You say no and then you come closer. Did you really think I'd let you walk by me, or were you hoping I wouldn't?"

The possessiveness in his touch caused a feminine re-action to coil inside her, the same feeling she'd had when he'd tugged at the lace of her dress. An excited, curious sense of the inevitable poured through her veins. She lifted her chin, looked into his eyes and covered the truth with half a lie. "Perhaps I was. You're still an at-tractive man, Joel." She couldn't move, couldn't breathe. She could only wait to see what he would do next.

"Ever the truthful scientist. You're an excellent teacher, Alison." The sensuous curve of his mouth matched the bittersweet, husky tone. "How are you as a pupil?"

"That depends on the subject matter."

"You're leading with your chin, sweetheart."

One knuckle lay against her skin, its warmth burn-ing her. "With you, I always have."

Holding her eyes with his, he pulled her closer. "Did you think you were leading with your chin when you came to New York City to see me the second time?"

"I didn't come to see you. I came to see Tracy—"

"You, Ms Powell, are all wet. In more ways than one." Behind her water-slick head, the sky was splashed with the gold of the sunset, outlining her tilted chin, con-cealing her eyes.

To Alison, it seemed as if the world had stopped. He said, "We were good together once. We can be again."

"No."

His smile mocked her denial. "Yes, Alison." He tugged the towel from her hands, stripped it from her body and let it fall in a puddle at her ankles. She shivered in the cool night air. Instantly he wrapped her in his arms. She couldn't move, couldn't release herself from his warmth. She'd wanted it for too long. . . .

As he bent his head, the silk of his hair and his lips brushed her exquisitely sensitized skin.

"Please . . . don't. . . ."

Each word fell on Joel's ears like balm. Every syllable was a lovely, aching lie. He folded her wet body into his arms and bent his head to claim his prize.

Her mouth was hot, an exciting contrast to the coolness of her arms and shoulders. She smelled of water and the night, and he wanted to take her inside him, absorb her. The fiery, sweet taste of her mouth made him want more. He flattened his palm against her sleek, damp hip and pressed her closer, letting her feel the thrust of his body against hers.

She tensed momentarily, but his tongue curled out, wooing her with teasing passes at her lips. His other hand slid up to her nape, tangling in her hair. Had he really thought her skin chilled from the water? She was setting him on fire.

His heat surrounded Alison in a protective male warmth that was as seductive as satin sheets. Languor lay heavy in her bloodstream. She wanted to lie down, there on the dock, and have him lie with her. . . . "Please don't do this—"

His mouth caught the husky, halfhearted protest and turned it to his advantage, tasting, savoring the tiny opening with a playful thrust of his tongue that was withdrawn before she had time to respond. The curve of his mouth told her he was smiling. To be wooed with such tenderness and humor only tightened the silken bands around her.

Warm and smooth his mouth was, like cream, too rich to be consumed. Against her softness he was hard strength, long, sheathed muscles finding their place in preparation for loving. His fingers teased down her bare spine; a thigh nudged between hers.

"Joel—"

He wrapped his other leg behind her, trapping her, and threaded his hands deeper into her hair. Freed of all restraint, it poured over his fingers. Her head locked in place inches from his, he murmured, "Alison," in a mocking echo of her whisper. "Take a chance. Step off the end of the world with me. Be brave." Smiling, he fit his lips to hers once more.

To Alison, it seemed as if he'd called up every unfair advantage at his command. She leaned back, taking her mouth from his. "Being brave is one thing. Being foolhardy is another."

He laughed, as she had known he would. Thinking she'd distracted him, she relaxed, only to have his mouth boldly recapture what he'd lost. All those feelings were there still, magnified a hundredfold by his absence from her life.

Joel was more than ready to nurture her need, feed her hunger. With hands and arms he cradled and comforted her even while he aroused her. He teased her with his tongue, retreating slightly and then advancing with more boldness to delve more deeply, to taste and explore more of the treasure. He touched her tongue, flicking at it. With all the velvet delight of her mouth given willingly into his possession, he was free to woo her in whatever way he chose.

Deliberately he deepened the rhythm, until he was kissing her in the most erotic way a man can kiss a woman.

She was feminine and beautiful and yielding, and he knew that if he didn't draw away soon, he would confirm her conviction that he was a man who needed sexual satisfaction from her and nothing more. He braced himself for the jolt that would come when he stopped kissing her; slowly he lifted his mouth. Her lips were beautifully swollen, her eyes dark and aroused. "You're a quick study, Alison. But as I recall . . . you always were." His drawl mocked her, conjured up nights when she'd run to him eagerly and mornings when she'd awakened in his arms. "Come back to my cabin with me."

She wanted to go; she ached to go. But a cooler, saner voice said, *He rejected you once, and you put yourself back together. Could you do it again?*

She lifted her head. "No, Joel," she said steadily.

"Cautious, clever Alison. Why is it that when I'm kissing you I forget you have that cautious streak?" He gazed at her speculatively. "And why is it that I keep wondering what it would take to make you forget your caution?"

Leaving her to stare after him in the gathering darkness, he turned and walked away. Under her feet, the dock vibrated from the shock of his going. And so did she.

6

A LOON FRANTICALLY beat its wings to keep its heavy body tilted in an intolerable position, suspended between air and water, then tipped its rear down to splash to a landing on the lake. Alison's class elbowed one another, jockeying for position along the dock for a clear view. She bit back her cautioning words, hoping their enthusiasm would hold. In the afternoon sun, the sky snapped with blue clarity and the lake glowed like a sapphire gem. The day couldn't have been more perfect if she'd written the specifications into her lesson plans. Even the loon was cooperating. Out on the water, the bird floated with quiet assurance, its head cocked to allow it to keep an eye on the rowdy bunch of humans on shore.

"Look, he sees us," a girl said excitedly. "He's not afraid. He's coming closer."

"Maybe he's taking a class on humans," drawled Marty.

Over the boy's head, Alison met Joel's sober gaze. He looked exactly like Peck's bad boy trying to stifle a smile, amusement lurking in his eyes. She had controlled her urge to grin at Marty's quip, but at the sight of Joel, her mouth tilted. Joel matched her grin with his own outrageous smile. On the bank, away from the jostling crowd, his bare arms folded over his rumpled gray sweatshirt, he looked summer bronzed, far too masculine. Khaki shorts covered two inches more of his legs than the sweatshirt did.

She should have looked away instantly, but when she didn't, the expression in his eyes changed; the memory of the kiss they'd shared burned there. She swung away to look out over the water, her cheeks warm. She couldn't go on like this, half her mind involved with Joel, the other half with her class.

"Is that what we're supposed to be looking for, that bird in the black-checkered suit?" Jennifer said, and giggled. A look from Kathryn made her subside into silence. Ted nudged a boy named John with his elbow, knocking him sidewise to the edge of the dock, where he teetered and would have splashed into the water if Marty hadn't caught his arm.

So much for high-minded ideals. If Alison was going to teach them anything at all, she'd have to get them to use their cleverness for something besides badgering one another. "Everybody sit down."

Instantly a forest of knees sprouted on the dock. The kids propped their notebooks in their laps. For good measure, Marty crossed his eyes as well, clowning. "We're supposed to look for boids?" It was a Jerry Lewis face and a voice to match. Grinning, Marty twisted his head to look at Joel, asking for approval. From his place at the side of the hill, Joel shot him a warning look. Marty's eyes uncrossed, and his mouth closed.

I have to get his secret, Alison thought.

After two weeks of classes, group dynamics had taken over. The others had picked friends, but Marty remained the odd man out, whether by his choice, Alison didn't know. Joel was the only one to whom Marty had formed an attachment.

Joel stood watching, his eyes on the strange bird, his mind on Alison. She seemed quiet today, more subdued. Had he made any headway at all last night? He thought he had. He didn't know what she was thinking or feeling. He only knew it was cruel and unusual punishment to look at her today. Her T-shirt fitted her nicely; her shorts exposed long, shapely legs. She was one of the few women he'd ever seen who looked good in white sneakers. Actually, she looked good any time of the day or night, wet or dry. Last night her hair had been dark and wet. Today the sun caught in the red-gold locks, making them burn like wildfire. Joel sat down on the grassy bank, his eyes on the shimmering water ahead of him.

His movement brought Alison's eyes to him. He was leaning back on his hands, his long, muscular legs stretched out in front of him, his feet crossed at the ankles. She remembered how that body had felt pressed against her wet one last evening. The thought of that had kept her awake most of the night....

"What would anyone like to know about the loon?" This was her new approach, her attempt to elicit curiosity from her students.

To her surprise and pleasure, questions flew at her fast and furiously. Was a loon a duck? Where did it live and what did it eat?

"Common loons are not ducks. They're in the same class, *aves*, as are all birds, but they belong to the order of *gaviiformes*. Ducks, swans and geese are in an order called *anseriformes*."

"Loons live like the rich and famous. They winter along southern ocean coasts and summer in Canada or the northern United States. A mating pair will return to the same location they summered at the year before, just like some of your parents return to their campsites here."

"What are their nests like?"

Alison directed her gaze back to the bird bobbing on the water. "Loons require a special combination of wetlands and marsh for nesting. Every time a marshy area next to a body of water is drained by man to erect houses or condominiums, loons lose a nesting place. Naturalists are beginning to be concerned, fearing that the loon may become an endangered species. They're fish eaters, which also makes them vulnerable to air and water pollution. If fish absorb pollutants, those same irritants are absorbed by the loon."

"Look, he's gone," one boy said. "He went under the water. Isn't he ever going to come up?"

"Loons are excellent divers and can stay underwater for several minutes, searching for food."

Casually, as if he didn't really care about the answer, Marty asked, "Why is he out there all alone? Are loons loners?"

She glanced at Marty to see if he was up to his usual tricks, playing word games, but the boy was sitting staring out over the water at the bird, his face drawn and serious. It was then that she understood. He felt a kinship with that solitary loon. Over the boy's head, Alison's eyes met Joel's. "That's an excellent observation, Marty," she said in a light tone. "In the spring and summer, loons *are* loners. They feed alone or with their mates rather than traveling in flocks as ducks and geese do. In the winter, though, they congregate in flocks."

The dark head with its slender black bill appeared above the water. Watching the bird, Alison asked her students to list the sayings they knew that had "loon" in them. They enjoyed rattling them off, Looney Tunes cartoons and "loony" as a slang synonym for "crazy."

"Actually, the association between loony and crazy comes through the word 'lunar,' which means moon. In the past, people believed that looking at a full moon for too long could cause insanity. Hence, loony. As you can see, those sayings have nothing to do with the common loon."

They spent another hour talking about the loon, and while they talked the loon floated closer, curling its head and diving repeatedly, performing for them like a ballet star onstage. Alison couldn't have asked for a more cooperative subject. Toward the end of the hour, it even tilted its head and delivered its unearthly and distinctive hooting cry.

Influenced by the antics of the loon and her own more relaxed presentation, Alison's students, especially those two or three who were bent on looking "cool," dropped their blasé poses. By the end of the class, the unique bird with its checkered coat, its graceful dive and its haunting call had enthralled them.

When the loon decided it was time to fly away, they couldn't believe how the bird churned the water with its webbed feet, almost as if it were walking on the surface, before lifting its body into the air. While the thump of its heavy, rapid wing beats echoed in their ears, they craned their necks to keep sight of it until the last possible moment.

It had been a good session, and Alison was reluctant to see it end. Still caught in the spell of the afternoon and the feeling that she'd imparted something of the wonder and uniqueness of the loon to her students, she nodded to them, indicating they were free to go back to the campground.

As if the hour of intense concentration had never been, they exploded into life and scrambled to their feet. In the confined area of the dock, Ted stumbled against Tom. Incensed that his space had been violated, Tom whirled around to deliver retribution to the other boy and accidently caught Kathryn in the side with his elbow just as she was getting to her feet. She lost her balance, toppled over the edge of the dock and landed with a splash in the water.

After that, everything was a blur. Marty's face, rosy with fury, flashed into Alison's vision. He called Tom a name, slung a fist in the general direction of the boy's middle and then jumped into the water. Alison ran to the side, ready to jump in after him, when a hand gripped her arm. "Let him go," Joel said in her ear.

"But he can't swim!"

"Kathryn can. And she seems to know lifesaving. Look."

Alison looked. Joel was right. Kathryn was swimming easily with Marty in a classic lifesaving hold, her hand under his chin. "Don't grab me," Alison heard the girl cry. "Just lie back and let me hold your head up." Kicking, splashing, choking, the boy obeyed.

Regaining her wits, Alison ordered the rest of the class to head for the cafeteria to catch their bus. "They're all right," she said as several worried faces turned to her. "They're fine. Go on before you miss your bus."

They were reluctant to walk away from the dramatic happening, but Alison ordered them in her best authoritative-teacher voice to go, and they went, trudging up the hillock.

Relieved, Alison turned her attention back to the two in the lake. Kathryn had tugged Marty to the dock. He grasped a rung and thrashed onto his stomach. Joel extended a hand to him and none too gently hauled him over the side to sit on the dock. Kathryn followed, her dark-black hair and shorts dripping, her blouse clinging to her young breasts.

"Why on earth did you jump in after her when you can't swim?" Alison asked, her heart thumping when she thought about what could have happened if Kathryn had been less coolheaded and less skilled.

Marty had the sense to look foolish. In an effort to recapture his poise, he sat up straighter and ran a hand over his carroty hair, slicking the moisture out of it. "I didn't want her to be alone."

Alison opened her mouth, but Joel's hand gripped her arm, cautioning her. He was looking at Kathryn.

She was standing in front of Marty. Gracefully she leaned over and held out her hand to help him up. Apparently in a daze, he took it. She brought him to his feet and then said, "It was nice of you to worry about me, Marty."

"No problem." It was such a blatant male attempt to shrug off his own inability to swim and retain his pride that Alison wanted to laugh. Marty straightened his shoulders and tried to regain his blasé face, but his emotions betrayed him. It was obvious Kathryn's words had pleased him; he was having to work hard to keep the smile off his face.

Alison looked at the two of them, thinking they both resembled drowned rats. Jeans, sneakers, T-shirts were sodden. "I can't let you go home on the bus like this—"

"I'll take them home." Joel stepped forward and reached for Kathryn's hand. He helped her off the dock, then turned to Marty. "Come on, ace. I already know where you hang out."

"We've moved. We're on Rollins Pond." Marty's voice was tight, his eyes on Joel's hand holding Kathryn's.

"That's where my family is now, too." Kathryn flashed a smile at Marty.

"Fine," Joel drawled. "I'll run my own private bus."

"Wait." Alison came off the dock toward him. "I'd better go with you and explain to their parents what happened. Let me get some towels from my cabin, and I'll meet you at yours." She looked at the two dripping teenagers. "Go with Joel. And stay away from the water."

Marty grinned. "Afraid we might get wet, teach?"

Alison stared back at him, more afraid of what she would have done to him if she hadn't been a responsible teacher.

"YOUR BACK SEAT is going to be damp for a while."

"It's a rental car. Let the company worry about it."

Alison and Joel had dropped the teenagers and were on their way back to their camp. Marty's parents hadn't been at the family site, but Kathryn's had. When they'd learned that their daughter had taken a tumble into the lake and then had had to rescue her would-be lifesaver, they had laughed and teased her until she'd turned a charming pink.

The best part—or the worst—had been sitting in the front seat listening to Kathryn and Marty make tentative conversation in the back. Kathryn had been serious, Marty wisecracking to cover up his nervousness. The two of them, with their shy reaching out to each other through words, had reminded Alison of herself and Joel that first summer.

It was not a comfortable thought. Alison laid her head on the headrest, thinking this had been a long day.

She must have dozed, for it seemed like only an instant later when Joel pulled up in front of her cabin. How could she have relaxed enough in his company to sleep? Yet it seemed she had. Her restless night and the strain of the day had caught up with her. In her semiconscious state, she knew only one thing. She didn't want him to go. "Would you like to come in?"

In the silent, golden light of the late afternoon, his face was a dark, unfathomable mask. He turned and reached for her face, catching her chin in his hand to bring her head around. "For what?" He met her gaze head-on, boldly.

"For coffee. For supper. For talk."

His lean fingers caressed her skin, his eyes mocking her offer. "I don't want coffee or supper or talk."

Her body reacted to the dark invitation in his eyes, her breasts lifting and swelling against her cotton shirt. He drew his finger down her cheek, his smile headily intimate. "You're looking at me as if I were one of your students who just gave you the wrong answer."

"You are, and you did."

"I'm not the one who keeps giving the wrong answer—you are. You keep saying no." His hand strayed to her hair. "Actually, I'm teasing you, sweet." He curled a strand around her ear, his touch on that delicate shell of skin warm, disturbing. "I thank you for your kind offer, but I have other plans."

"I thought you had Monday evenings off from the club."

He looked at her thoughtfully. "I do."

"I . . . see." Her eyes flickered away. She had no right to ask Joel where he was going or what he was doing. No right at all.

"Do you? I doubt it." The twist of his mouth, the cool distancing in his eyes reminded her of Marty. What had she said to make him raise pride as a barrier? Feeling alone and hurt by his rejection, she swung her legs out of the car and closed the door behind her. As she murmured goodbye and heard his mocking farewell, she was still wondering what she'd said to displease him.

Thinking of how she'd looked, Joel drove too fast down the curving road. She thought he was going to see another woman. It had been written all over her face, her lovely face, and in her averted blue eyes. His mood dark, he was deep in thought and nearly missed the turn into the state camping park that was his destination.

When he pulled up at the campsite, where only an hour before he'd dropped Marty, his mood was not good. He clamped down on his temper and prepared himself to speak to Marty's mother.

Luckily for his state of mind, she was receptive to his plan. Joel asked where the boy was then and was directed to a clearing across the road. He strode into the pines to find Marty sitting on the stump of a tree, idly cracking peanuts, tossing them on the ground along with the shells. At the snap of a twig under Joel's foot, Marty jumped. He saw Joel, and his eyebrows came together in a frown. "What are you doing here?"

"I came to see you."

"What for?"

"It's time you learned to swim."

Marty swore.

Joel kept his expression blank, as if he hadn't heard. "Not here. We'll go to the beach at Fish Creek."

Marty's eyes widened slightly at Joel's sensitivity. He wouldn't have to make a fool of himself in full view of his stepfather's campsite. "I'm not going."

"Would you like to make a little bet on that?"

"My mother—"

"I've already spoken to your mother. Now, are you going to come under your own steam, or shall I help you?"

CLIMBING OUT OF THE CAR and walking over the sand to the water at Fish Creek beach, Joel had a feeling his patience would be sorely tried before the evening was over. But once he got the boy in the water, Marty surprised him. The youngster gave his full attention to the effort. He did exactly as Joel said, and by the end of the evening, when they were both turning blue with chill, Marty was floating on his stomach, turning his head and breathing. He hadn't yet mastered the coordination of his arms and legs, but it would take only another lesson or two before Marty would be able to swim, at least for a short distance.

ALISON STOOD in the darkening shadows of the birch trees, watching the man work patiently with the boy. She saw Joel shake his head, tow Marty into shallow water, heard him say, "Try it again. Come on now. This time blow the water out of your nose, don't breathe it in."

She felt as if she couldn't breathe herself. She might have been watching two strangers, yet that dark head bent over Marty's splashing arms was as familiar to her as her own.

You're not playing fair, Joel Brandon. It's not fair to make me feel like this, not fair to take my heart and

wring it with your caring for this kid, who has as much
appeal as a porcupine.

She hadn't meant to spy on him. After she'd eaten her
evening meal she'd grown restless, thinking about
Marty and Kathryn, and she'd driven to Marty's
campsite to talk to his mother, only to discover that
Marty had been whisked away by Joel for a swimming
lesson. Driving back along the winding road that
curved past the campsites, she had slowed at the path
that shot off toward the beach. She had swung the
wheel and taken it. And now she was standing in the
shadow of a silvery clump birch, wishing she hadn't.

Joel Brandon had the capacity for love; he just didn't
know it. And concealing herself, watching him, Alison
discovered that her capacity for loving *him* was a million times greater than she'd ever dreamed.

Purple clouds drifted across the sky. The sun was
dropping, and so was the temperature. Even while
Alison felt the first chill of the night touch her skin, Joel
pulled Marty to his feet. Man and boy stood in the
waist-high water. Joel gestured toward the shore, evidently telling his pupil it was time to go. Marty was
shaking his head. Joel turned his back on the boy and
began to splash toward the shore. Marty stood looking after him, then turned and lunged into a clumsy
swimmer's crawl, heading straight for deep water.

"No," Alison whispered, proud of the boy's courage
yet afraid he was getting in too deep and that Joel
wouldn't see him until it was too late. She was just ready
to step out of hiding and cry out to Joel, when he
turned, saw what was happening and curved his arms

over his head to do a swift, shallow dive that took him to the boy's side. Like a shark picking up its prey, Joel whipped the boy around and hauled him to his feet in the shallower water. Joel stumbled onto the beach with Marty in tow.

Caught between the urge to laugh and cry, Alison shrank back into the shadow of the trees, not wanting to break the intimacy between man and boy. Joel had evidently learned his own lesson: not to turn his back on his student. His hand was shackled to Marty's arm. His feet covered with white sand, his hair dripping, he snatched up the towels that lay in readiness, wrapped one around Marty and pushed him forward. With the boy stumbling through the sand ahead of him, Joel strode by Alison, his face dark with annoyance.

Neither male looked her way. When they'd climbed into Joel's car and gone, Alison turned and walked through the darkening night to her own car, her heart so full of conflicting emotions she couldn't sort them all out. Except one. An overwhelming tenderness.

THE NIGHT RUSTLED AND SIGHED around her as she walked down the path to Joel's cabin. The air was cool on her arms, but her skin burned with excitement. The breeze seemed to whisper a warning. Alison ignored it and went on picking her way through the trees. Slivers of moonlight, sliced by the tall pines, were laid at her feet, illuminating the path ahead of her. She'd exchanged her sneakers for sandals, and fallen needles crunched underfoot.

The sound didn't match the rise and fall of her own feet. Someone . . . or something . . . was coming down the path toward her.

Alison's heart leaped into her throat. A vision of a bear, the one Joel had described, danced in front of her eyes. She began to run. The crackle of the needles told her it was too late. She was being chased, attacked. All they'd find in the morning would be a scrap of her T-shirt and a little fingernail. From the sound of him, he was gigantic—

"What in the devil are you doing, training for the Olympics?"

Angry, frightened, embarrassed, she whirled on the dark figure: Joel. "What are you doing out here?"

In the silence that followed, all she could hear was her own tortured breathing and the pounding of her heart in her ears. Then Joel's voice, silky, mocking. "What are *you* doing out here?"

She fought to control her raspy breathing. "I was coming to . . . see you—to talk to you," she added hastily.

In the darkness, his hair looked black, his face smooth. Suddenly he bent toward her, his nose between her shoulder and neck. He breathed in deeply, inhaling the clean scent of her hair and the perfume she'd splashed on in a gesture of bravado. "For a woman who's only coming to talk to a man, you certainly were lavish with scent."

"I dropped the perfume bottle." Recovering, nodding at the one he carried, she said, "You seem to have brought your bottle along."

He released his steadying grip on her arm and lifted the bottle in acknowledgement. "I was coming to offer you a goodbye drink."

"Goodbye?"

"Yes. As in fond farewell, bon voyage, et cetera."

"I see."

"Do you?" he asked in an echo of his words that afternoon. The pines sighed an accompaniment to his soft tone.

"More than you think."

He was silent for a moment, and she wondered if he'd heard her. Then he lifted the bottle and gestured with it. "Well, which way? Forward to yours or back to mine?"

"It's closer to mine."

"Yours it is, then."

He dropped behind to follow her along the narrow path. Her breathing had slowed somewhat, but her pulse was accelerating, in anticipation now. He was leaving. It was what she had once wanted desperately. And now she didn't want it at all.

He was still behind her when they climbed the cabin steps. She pulled open the door and held it for him. When he was inside, she rushed forward and snatched up the clothes she'd tossed to the floor, her shorts and T-shirt, the bra and pants she'd stripped out of and replaced with clean ones. "Sorry. I wasn't expecting you to come here." She stuffed the dirty clothes in the pillowcase she used as a laundry bag while he stood watching her, the bottle in his hand.

"Please. Make yourself at home." She gestured at the table. "I'll get glasses."

It seemed odd to Joel to sit down at the table while she made a lie of her words, ignored him and went on fussing around the cabin, self-consciously pulling up the comforter on the bed and picking up a damp towel. He felt strange, irritated and wonderful all at the same time. He stretched his legs to one side of the table and said, "Alison. I'm not your mother. You don't have to tidy up the place for me."

She'd been tucking the comforter into the foot of the bed. She straightened suddenly and looked at him, her face flushed, her eyes dark. "No, of course you aren't, and I don't, and I'm not." Having said that, she went back to straightening the bed as if they'd never spoken.

He shook his head, but a smile played over his lips as he got out of the chair and opened the cupboard to pluck out two glasses. He poured a small amount for Alison and a more generous share into his glass. His eyes on her, he put the glasses on the table and settled into the chair again.

Leaning over the bed, Alison sliced a hand under the pillow, making the cover taut. Aware of his gaze on her, she turned and looked around the room. The clothes were gone, the bed made. There was nothing more for her to do.

Brown eyes that looked nearly black in the lamplight followed her as she approached the table. She sank into the chair across from him, tucking her legs to one side to avoid his long ones, picking up her glass. With the air of Socrates swallowing hemlock, she drank. It was brandy, and the heady liquor burned all the way down her throat. She didn't cough, but she wanted to badly.

"I suggest you go a little easy on that stuff. As I remember, you're not a heavy drinker."

She set down the glass and tried to match his look of casual blandness. "Perhaps your memory is faulty."

His eyes caught hers, held. "Not likely. I remember most things very well." He fingered the glass, watching her in that disturbing way he had, and she knew as if he'd said it aloud that what he remembered very well was making love to her. "You said you wanted to talk to me."

"What I had to say isn't important now." Unable to go on looking at him, she broke eye contact.

"If I had to guess—" he twirled the glass idly on the table, his interest seemingly captivated by the swirls of moisture on the green-painted tabletop "—I'd say you were coming over to ask me to leave. But since I said I was going, you prefer not to add insult to injury by telling me something you no longer feel is necessary for me to know." He lifted the glass and looked at her over it. "Am I close?"

"Amazingly so," she lied, wondering where the perfidious woman had come from who seemed to be residing in her skin.

"There's just one hole in my reasoning. Why would a woman use scent when she was coming to tell a man she wanted him out of her life?"

She lifted her glass and flashed a brave smile at him. "How much of this stuff have you had?"

"Not enough," he said with feeling.

She knew what he meant. He meant he hadn't had enough to dull the pain of wanting her. Nor had she. To sustain her courage, she took another swallow. It seemed desperately important to stop him from going, but she hadn't the faintest idea how to do it without sounding silly or stupid or throwing herself at him. And she was afraid, terribly afraid, that he was leaving because that was what he really wanted to do.

"What about Marty? Are you just going to walk off and leave him—" She nearly said, 'Too,' but she caught herself.

"Marty's a survivor. He'll live."

"I saw you with him tonight at the beach." That brought his eyes to her face. "For a man who's...rarely taught anyone anything before, you were very good with him."

"Thank you." His lashes dropped. "I find I'm not up to your standard."

"You're the first person who's broken through to him since his friend died."

"You were watching the whole time?"

"Most of it."

He raised his eyes, pinned her with his dark gaze. "May I ask where you were?"

She lifted her glass and smiled. Her pain had gone away. There was nothing left but a lovely haze. "You may. I was hiding. Behind a tree."

"Clever of you."

"Yes, wasn't it?"

"Then you must have seen me turn my back on him long enough to nearly let him drown."

"One of the first lessons a teacher learns. Never turn your back on your students. Especially ones whose names begin with *M*."

"I'll remember that." He lifted his glass and drained it. When he set it down, he faced her and said in a cool tone, "It's not often a man gets to drown his sorrows in the company of the woman who drove him to drink." He rose, dipped his head, bowed in a courtly fashion and then stood looking at her. She couldn't begin to guess his thoughts. "Thank you for your forbearance. Now I think it's time for me to go."

She clenched her hands together in her lap, took a breath and gathered all the courage she had. Then she raised her eyes to his. "I wasn't going to ask you to leave, Joel. I was going to ask you if you still . . . wanted me."

He stood very, very still. "I've never stopped wanting you." He waited, his eyes locked with hers. When she said nothing, only swallowed, he said softly, a smile on his lips, "Don't lose your courage now, sweet."

His soft voice and the look on his face were not much incentive, but they were all she had. "Would you like to . . . stay?"

7

JOEL PUT A HAND on the chair he'd just vacated and rested his hip on the corner of the table, his movements so easy that for a moment she thought he'd mistaken her meaning. When she met his eyes, she knew he hadn't. "I'd like that very much." Still he waited. The silence crackled between them as if the air were electrically charged. In the same abbreviated sweatshirt and shorts that he'd worn to class that afternoon, he looked lean, masculine, one long, sinewy leg crossed over the other. "Are you sure that's what you want?" A lifted eyebrow punctuated the husky question.

"Yes," she said quickly, too quickly.

He gazed thoughtfully at her. "No, I don't think it is. You may think so now, but..."

Joel slid off the table, knowing that if he didn't leave soon, he would accept the sweet temptation of her. Even now he could feel his body urging him to go to her, to lift her from the chair and lock her in his arms. When he turned to look at her, he saw that her face was flushed with embarrassment and distress.

"Alison—"

"Don't...apologize." She shoved the glass of brandy away with the back of her hand. "You men aren't the only ones who dislike pity." She raised her heated face to him. "You've changed your mind. It's...all right. I'll survive. Now just go."

"I haven't changed my mind. I just don't understand why you've changed yours."

"You don't have to understand me. You don't have to understand anything about me. Just . . . go." She stood and collected his tumbler and her own. In her unsteady hands, the glasses clinked together, sounding like thunder in her ears. He didn't move. She moved away to put them in the sink, and knowing it would take more strength than she had to turn and watch him walk out the door, she kept her back to him and braced her hands on the counter, waiting until the creak of the screen door told her he'd gone.

His warm hands slid around her middle, and she was brought back against him. A relief such as she had never known flooded every cell in her body.

"Alison."

She leaned her head against his shoulder, felt the strength of his chest against her back, the caress of his breath on her neck. There was everything she hoped for in that husky whisper of her name, a plea for forgiveness, a wealth of longing.

She covered the hands that were clasped in front of her with her own and told him with her touch that no forgiveness was needed, now that he held her in his arms. "My seduction technique leaves something to be desired, I know, but it's the best I could do on the spur of the moment." It was a shaky attempt at humor, but she needed to ease the tension between them.

"Your best is too damn good." He sounded shaken. "You must have known I wouldn't be able to walk out that door, even though it would be a million times better for you if I did."

Joel could feel the tension still tightening her body, and the thought of easing it brought tension of another kind to his.

"No, as a matter of fact, I was certain you would leave." She wanted this one wonderful moment of understanding to go on forever. If only the world would stop and she could stay locked in Joel's arms, knowing absolutely that he wanted her more than he wanted to stay untouched and invulnerable.

As if he knew what she needed, he went on holding her, not kissing her, not moving his hands, just . . . holding her.

He stood inhaling the scent of her silky hair, feeling the slimness of her waist under his hands. Her breathing had accelerated slightly, and he knew his had, too. Outside, a passing breeze stirred the pine trees, and his senses reacted with spine-tingling awareness to the soughing wind and the shadowy cabin and the lovely woman who leaned against his chest. That delicious sense of anticipation just before he went taut with desire rippled through him.

Alison exhaled softly, a sigh of contentment and passion; his anticipation burgeoned into full-blown readiness. That quickly she brought him to aching need. He slipped his hands from beneath hers and brushed the taut underside of her breasts with his knuckles. She breathed in sharply and trembled. Her reaction sent another tremor of pleasure through him.

Just as he was going to turn her, she twisted in his arms and faced him, slipping her hands around his waist to bring him close once more. The lovely weight of her breasts pressed against his chest, and the cradle of her hips fit his with erotic precision. The fullness tightened. "Sweetheart, about the alleged inadequacy of your seduction technique . . ."

She lifted wise, delighted eyes to his face. "Yes?"

"Highly exaggerated."

"You have it on good authority?"

"The best. Although perhaps further investigation might uncover a hidden tendency toward evasiveness. . . ."

She slid her hands under the front of his sweatshirt and found the delicate nubs of his nipples. He inhaled abruptly. "No, no evasiveness. Just head-on assault."

Once, long ago, she'd learned about a man's body from him. With patience and humor he'd shown her exactly how and where to touch him. He'd done it in such a way that she had felt neither naive nor stupid. Now she added refinements to his instruction, gently rubbing her palms over his nipples, thrilling to the way they hardened under her caressing hands.

Groaning, he set about exacting his retribution. His lean fingers moved under her T-shirt, unfastened her wispy bra, pushed it aside to seek the warm, rounded flesh.

Alison had forgotten how insidiously soul destroying his touch could be, how gentle one moment and playful the next. She'd forgotten the way her breasts developed a sleek fluidity in his hands, how, like a sculptor, he seemed to turn her flesh into molten clay that responded to the slightest manipulation from his teasing fingers. "Joel . . ."

Her body heavy with languor, she arched to make her breasts more accessible to the lovely torture he meted out with relentless ease. He took advantage of her bared throat to fit his mouth to the vulnerable hollow, exploring it with great thoroughness, lashing her with his tongue, sending new and more devastating tremors darting through her.

Joel was driven. He wanted to wipe away her uncertainty, bring her such pleasure that whatever the aftermath of their loving, she would have no regrets. He sought and found her mouth, and as he again devoted himself to heightening her enjoyment, taking her lower lip gently between his teeth and exploring her lips with his tongue, he discovered something. For each sweet liberty he took, she gave him twice what he'd asked, and seeing to her enjoyment heightened his to an exquisite point that bordered on pain.

Carefully he lifted his mouth from hers and looked down into her dark, desire-hazed eyes. His must have been filled with the same deep hunger. Without a word, she grasped the bottom of her shirt to lift it over her head and gracefully shrug away her bra.

Her smooth, golden shoulders gleamed in the lamplight, and below the V of her collarbone, her breasts swelled, the peaks rosy and lifted. Joel swallowed, then started as he felt her hands lifting his shirt from his body.

They stood gazing at each other, just outside the ring of light that the lamp cast over the table. For Alison, the reality of seeing him exceeded her dreams and her memories. Dark, curly hair swirled around his nipples, drew a dark line down his flat stomach. His shoulders were muscular, golden with new tan. She ached to touch, to know. Deliberately she caught his shoulders with her hands and leaned against him, brushing her breasts to his warm skin. He stood as still as if she'd turned him to stone. Knowing instinctively that it was only his supreme control that kept him from surrendering to her, she continued to rub tiny circles against him as if she were a silky cat. He stood accepting her sweet torture until she enlarged the circles. His willpower collapsing, he emitted a low, throaty groan and swept her off her feet to carry her to the bed.

In one smooth motion, he reached for her hips in that warm nest of covers, divested her of her remaining clothes, then stood to take off his.

His eyes never left her face as he lay down beside her and pulled her into his arms. He bent his head and buried his mouth in the soft skin of her neck, almost as if seeking solace.

"If you hadn't been wearing this perfume I might have walked out that door. It was the only thing that gave me some hope that you really planned to come to me."

"I'll write the Arpège people a thank-you note."

"Will you?" He lifted away from her and looked into her eyes. "Are you sure you won't regret this?"

She wanted to make a quip, but the look in his eyes told her he was serious. "No, Joel, I won't regret this." Her dark-blue eyes played over his face. "What about you?"

"The only regret I have is that I can't—"

"Don't," she said, lifting her hand to close his lips. "Please...don't." She couldn't—wouldn't—listen to the excuses he might give for not loving her.

When he looked as if he was going to say something else, she dropped her head to his chest. Feeling as if she'd never touched him before, she explored the hair-crisped flesh with great concentration. When he reached for her, she shook her head. "No. I want you to lie back and let me . . . love you."

Something dark and dangerous flickered in his eyes at the word, but he did as she asked. She took time and care with his body, lingering here, sculpting there, circling his arms, teasing his fingertips, tracing his nose. Slowly, tenderly, her eyes on his, she brushed down the path of dark curling hair that led to his abdomen. When she closed her hand around him, his eyes seemed to smolder with flame. "Not inadequate at all," he muttered as she stroked the velvet softness of him, and his teeth clamped down on his lip while he fought for control.

This was not what Joel had expected. He hadn't expected her to make love to him with such feminine assurance and maturity. In the three years since he'd been with her, she'd changed. She was quintessential woman, exulting in her power over him. He should have been disturbed by her sureness, but he wasn't. Her strength only made him feel more masculine, more alive, more real. The world was a heady place, a place of vivid colors and intense joy, joy that Alison poured over him with such ease that she was driving him out of his mind. . . .

He grasped her hand and brought her astride him, her thighs an exquisite pleasure enclosing his. Yet he knew he must deny himself the ultimate ecstasy for a few moments longer. It was past time to return the pleasure she'd given him. He found her silky, feminine treasure and stroked it gently, enjoying her instant moan of satisfaction. He made love to her with the deep sense of completeness that comes from pleasure received and given. He loved everything about her. He loved the way her hair fell like roseate gold over her breasts. He loved the way her hips lifted over him in age-old impatience. And he loved the way her body covered his in the ultimate embrace.

His body slid easily into hers; he belonged to her and she to him. He began to move, and she cried out, bending over him to seek his mouth with hers. Soon, too soon, they erupted into molten heat too powerful to be denied any longer. . . .

JOEL STOOD against the wall in the dining hall the next afternoon, listening to the rain beating on the roof while he watched Alison teach her class indoors. And he faced the brutal truth. What had started as an amusing interlude in which he'd pursued a woman he wanted to take to bed had become something far more serious. He had thought he could touch her and leave his heart untouched. He'd been wrong, so wrong. She had become too important to him. The final irony was that in the end, he was the one who would suffer more. He could never make her his. She didn't belong in his life any more than he belonged in hers. If he hadn't known it before that afternoon, he did now.

Knowing she was out of his reach, he had never wanted her more than he did at that moment. She wore her standard working clothes, shorts and a shirt, but he couldn't take his eyes off her flushed face, her sparkling eyes, her flying red-gold hair.

She had forgotten he existed. She was caught up in playing Bombardment, a cross between scientific Trivial Pursuit and a snowball war. Questions were asked, and the team who failed to answer correctly was "bombarded" with crumpled newspaper balls like snowballs. The purpose of the game, it seemed to him, was to set everybody in the room screaming and jumping up and down. The noise and confusion faded from Joel's sight. His vision turned inward, to the events of the night before, and he remembered....

"What's that noise?" she had asked sleepily. In that dark hour after they'd made love, Joel had lain in bed, Alison dozing in his arms. On awakening, her voice had been languorous with satisfied desire.

"Thunder." He stroked her hair, feeling sated with her yet needing to touch her still.

"Thunder." She repeated the word sleepily, as if the sound of it were foreign to her. "Umm." She burrowed more deeply into his shoulder, and her deep, even breathing made him believe she'd gone to sleep again. He was wrong. A moment later she murmured, "What's that noise?"

"Rain."

"Rain? It doesn't sound like rain—"

"For a science teacher, you're certainly having trouble identifying natural phenomena."

"Maybe that's because my sensory perceptions are all filled up with you." Her declaration brought no response from him. In the darkness, she was suddenly afraid. Had she said too much, revealed too much?

Needing to touch him, she lifted her fingers to his face, where she traced the sensual droop of his mouth. "Why aren't you asleep?"

"Too noisy."

"The rain?"

"Uh-uh. You."

The dark amusement in his voice brought delight and relief. She chuckled and drew the sheet over her breast. Idly he slipped his hand between the cotton and the jutting mound, thinking of nothing other than the pleasure it gave him to touch her. His pleasure increased sharply when he felt her flesh hardening, responding.

"Joel . . ."

"Shh. This time it's my turn." He went on circling, teasing, enticing, and as she began to writhe, he pushed back the sheet and bent over her, using his mouth to create more havoc.

He meted out her punishment slowly. With meticulous attention to detail, he explored the inside of her elbow, the hollow of her shoulder, the small of her back. Just as she had wielded her feminine power over him earlier, he now pleasured her with a masculine assurance that he knew he'd never before enjoyed with any woman. He took her to the heights and then, because she returned so generously what he gave, he joined her there, shuddering as the old-new waves of ecstasy rolled over him.

"Airmobile."

Alison's voice firing questions at her students brought Joel back to the present. She'd drawn another paper strip from the coffee can. On each strip was a word identifying a scientific discovery she'd discussed during the past two weeks. Alternating between her two student teams, Alison asked for definitions. Anyone on the team could answer the question. If no one knew the answer, the other team fired one crumpled paper ball each at the losers; they, in turn, were required to collect the balls and put them in a big green plastic bag emblazoned with their team name. At the end of the game, the team with the most crumpled balls lost.

"The airmobile runs on supercooled, then superheated air that turns to gas. It's still in the experimental stage!" a girl shouted.

"Third eye."

"The pineal gland inside the brain secretes melatonin during nighttime darkness and is considered by some to be our third eye." Marty answered that and received a rewarding smile from Kathryn, who was on his team.

"American Stonehenge." The opposing team members looked at one another and exhorted someone to answer, but no one could.

With howls of glee, Marty and his teammates snatched up paper balls. Standing with their toes on a strip of masking tape Alison had put down as the foul line, they took aim at their fellow classmates. Alison joined in the fun, looking like a kid herself, wading into the thick of the battle, lobbing a paper ball at the offenders with a shout of laughter.

When the din had abated, she said, "American Stonehenge, ladies and gentlemen, is located at Poverty Point in Louisiana. The site is more than a mile across and three thousand years old." She thrust her hand into the bowl and drew out another slip of paper. "Tell me about whale love songs."

"They sound like jazz," Marty said. "They have beginning melodies, followed by new ones. Each whale builds his melody on a repeated theme."

Tom, the boy Marty had tussled with over Kathryn, shot him a dark look. Here, in a competitive situation, Marty's intellectual prowess was evident to all. It was unfortunate that he and Tom were on opposing teams, and even more unfortunate that both boys were developing an interest in Kathryn. The girl had been shooting shy smiles of approval Marty's way every time he answered a question, which encouraged him to take the initiative more and more. While Alison was glad he was getting approval from at least one quarter, she didn't like the look on Tom's face. Jealousy was a potent emotion among young males of this age, and most boys didn't have the self-assurance to handle it well.

Alison tried to quell her misgivings, her sense that the game was alienating Marty more than ever from his peers. She concentrated on keeping the action going. The hilarity and general chaos and her worries about Marty required most of her attention, but in her peripheral vision she saw Joel lounging against the wall. Despite the hubbub, she was conscious of every move he made.

He didn't make many. He stood propped against the wall with the stillness and ease of a male model, his legs crossed at the ankles, his hands relaxed at his sides. He was wearing jeans today, which covered his long legs but revealed their muscular strength. A long-sleeved plaid shirt protected his arms from the rainy coolness. Worst of all, his poker face protected him from emotional exposure. Alison ached to know what he was thinking.

She longed to recapture the intimacy of mind as well as body that she'd shared with him the night before, but from the moment he'd walked in the door, she'd seen that it was not to be. She had asked him to join in the game, but he'd refused.

She remembered how it had been that morning, when he had awakened beside her. "Coffee first, or a shower?" she'd asked, reaching up to smooth back the tangle of dark hair from his forehead.

He'd looked at her thoughtfully, his eyes languid. "You're asking me to make a decision this early? I'm usually just going to bed at this time of the morning."

"Coffee it is." She'd thrown back the covers and reached for her nightshirt, the closest thing she had to a robe. He'd caught her wrist and dragged her bare body back to his, breast to chest, giving her a shock of pleasure. Her enjoyment was short-lived.

"Don't bother with anything for me. I'll just get dressed and go."

"Out in the rain? Why?"

"Let's just say that a little teacher discretion is called for on the morning after."

She had felt it then, the first chill wind of his rejection. He wasn't worried about her reputation—why should he be? There was no one there to care or see what she did. "Don't go sloshing back down the trail on my account." She leaned her arms on his chest, watching his eyes, knowing it was simply early-morning intimacy he didn't want. He had let himself be vulnerable to her last night, and his abrupt leave-taking that morning had been his way of rebuilding his defenses.

Shaking his head, he had lifted her gently aside. Then he'd crawled out, leaving her alone in the bed. As she watched him pull on his khaki shorts and shrug into his sweatshirt, she was filled with love and despair in equal amounts. In the cool, predawn gray light, he was hiding his body in his clothes and his mind in his silence. Caught in the throes of her own pride and hurt, his warmth still surrounding her in the nest of sheets, she was unwilling to break the silence in a futile attempt to make him stay. When he told her goodbye and turned to go, she said nothing to stop him. She couldn't. Her throat was too full of tears.

Did he feel her distress? She couldn't have said. Something, she didn't know what, made him pause at the doorway. He turned back, the expression in his eyes hidden, and said soberly that he'd see her in class. But when he walked out the door, she lay alone in the bed and wondered if he would take to his heels and flee to the city, as he'd originally planned. Seeing him walk in the dining-hall door that afternoon at the appointed time had filled her with such relief that her knees had gone shaky.

The team captains emptied the paper balls from the plastic bags onto the floor and counted them. Marty's side won, just as Alison had suspected it would. The victory celebration consisted of chocolate-chip cookies and cans of soda pop, the winners serving the losers. When she came around with the tray to Joel, he refused both. Despite her low-voiced request that he come and sit at a table with her, he remained where he was, standing against the wall. Only Marty seemed to notice his withdrawal, his eyes shifting to Joel at regular intervals. Even Kathryn's obvious preference for Marty's company didn't distract the boy from frequently twisting on the bench to glance back at Joel's face.

Marty cracked a joke, and both Alison and Kathryn laughed. Alison was where she belonged, thought Joel, here with this bunch of yet-to-be-civilized youngsters. She was one of the ones who would civilize them. This was her life, and there was no room in it for him. But even as he stood there watching her create an atmosphere of warmth, caring and learning with her students, he wanted her more than ever. He couldn't leave her. Not yet.

Alison didn't know what Joel was thinking; she only knew that the thought brought a frown. She had wanted him to join in the game and had been disappointed when he'd refused. She'd come up with the idea because of him, really. His observation that laughter heightens learning had set her mind working. The idea for the game had popped into her head one morning soon after that. She would tell him that he'd been the inspiration for the zany afternoon . . . if she got the chance to be alone with him again.

JUST AFTER MIDNIGHT, in the cool, whispering, rain-wet darkness, Joel pulled his rental car up in front of his cabin, got out and slammed the door. Deaf and blind to the dewed beauty of the night, he ran lightly up the cabin steps. It was late, and he was in a foul mood. The rain had prevented his giving Marty another swimming lesson, which hadn't pleased him. His act at the club had gone reasonably well considering he'd been only half-concentrating on it. He was in the enviable position of having a reputation that worked for him. People looked at him and expected to laugh. He no longer had to prove himself every time he walked on-stage. Joel had been quick to understand the crowd dynamic and capitalize on it. He had learned to relax, and his routines had become even more satirical, more outrageous. His success had snowballed. He'd recently been touted as one of the three best comedians in the country.

He didn't feel humorous at the moment. When he'd finally finished his last stint and realized it was too late to go to Alison's cabin unannounced, his mood had taken a definite plunge. His own damned stiff-necked pride had kept him from making plans with her before he'd left her that morning. Knowing he would have to sleep alone brought a curse to his lips. And knowing how desperately he needed her and how powerless he was to stop wanting her made him even more irritable.

He yanked open the door to his cabin, the thought of how he ached to be with her grating on him like sandpaper. He reached for the light switch, flipping it up absently. Nothing happened. The switch clicked, but he was still in the dark. The light bulb had died, making it the perfect ending to a bad day.

A soft, crackly paper missile hit him in the face. A second followed, passing his ear. Another crumpled paper ball bounced off his knee.

He faced into the dark and said, "I take it I'm on the losing team."

"Not yet." Another paper ball bounced off his shoulder. "You haven't been asked the question." Alison's voice floated out of the darkness to waft over his skin like that perfume of hers, sweeping away his foul mood in a flood tide of gladness. "Will you let me stay?" Her tone was half bravado, half apprehension.

He should tell her no. He should send her home. "Yes," he said. Then in a silky tone, "What do I get for giving the right answer? The teacher?"

There was a silence. "How about a chocolate-chip cookie?"

"That's all there is for the winner's spoils?" His voice was thick with mock disappointment.

Another pause. "There might be other... rewards offered." Her laughter was husky, seductive.

"I assume you were the one who tampered with my lamp."

"What powers of scientific deduction you have. Actually, I'm holding the light bulb hostage."

"I also assume you are not going to surrender your booty without... negotiation."

"Another correct answer. You're doing very well, Mr. Brandon."

"I may be doing well with the questions, but I can't see a damn thing. If it isn't too much trouble, would you give me directions?"

"Turn left at the first couch. I'm in your bed. That's the best place to indulge in chocolate-chip cookies... among other things."

"What an original concept." In the dark, he rolled into the bed, reached for her and pulled her under him, tangling her bare legs with his. She wore shorts and some kind of halter thing that he was going to have to investigate. He bent his head to kiss her . . . and had the crusty edge of a cookie thrust into his mouth.

"Nourishment first."

"Exactly what I was thinking." He brushed aside the cookie with one hand and smoothed the other over her chest, finding and cradling one cotton-covered breast in his palm. Her sudden, indrawn breath gave him an electric spark of pleasure.

His eyes were adjusting to the dark, and he could see the lovely outline of her face. He bent again to taste her lips. She twisted her head on the pillow, laughing at his mock growl of displeasure. His warm breath fanned her face, and she said, "You've been drinking. You'd better have something to eat." Again she pressed the cookie against his mouth. "Imbibing alcohol depletes all kinds of nutrients from the body, thiamine, calcium, vitamin D—"

"What a font of information you are. I had one small glass of Drambuie. Surely that's not enough to cause a full-blown case of malnutrition in two hours." But he found himself nibbling bites from the cookie she held because he knew it would please her. Her playfulness pleased him. After thinking about how much he wanted her, finding her in his bed filled him with joy. If she'd been like the uptight, status-conscious women he'd occasionally dated, she would never have come to his cabin eager and ready to make love to him, not without the standard ritual of advance and retreat.

Warmed to the depths of his soul, Joel munched the cookie, his hand cupping her pliable, feminine flesh. It was a new excursion into sensuousness for him to cuddle with a woman and be fed a sweet chocolate munchie from her hand while her body responded to his touch. He was wallowing in an unlikely mingling of satiation and desire.

Alison was playing a dangerous game, she knew. She had come determined to establish intimacy, to make him see that there was nothing dangerous about letting her into his life. She was acting on instinct, letting her mind fly free. If he wouldn't stay and talk with her in the morning, she would talk to him tonight. She'd created the dark purposely. In the dark, he would be off guard. He wouldn't have to shield his emotions from her. That was the theory. She only hoped it proved to be true.

"How did it go tonight at the club?"

"Routine." He finished the cookie and brought her fingers up to his mouth to nibble playfully at their tips.

"Biting the hand that feeds you is not the best of table manners."

"We're not at the table." He pressed her palm against his lips and used his tongue to trace an erotic line in the warm center.

Alison had expected resistance from him. She hadn't expected her own body to act the traitor to her campaign. She realized now that her preparations, hurrying through the dew-sweet forest, unscrewing the bulb with trembling fingers and scrambling into his bed to lie there in delicious anticipation, had heightened her sensual readiness. Warmth flowed through her veins, making her want to forget her scheme and simply lie back and let those wonderful hands touch her everywhere. "Was there a good crowd?"

He took the palm he had wet with his tongue and slid it under his shirt, pressing her smooth flesh against his hair-covered chest. "Moderate for a Tuesday. What are you doing?" He could feel her body stretching next to his, her hand reaching.

"Getting you another cookie."

He reached through the dark, caught her arm and brought her empty hand to rest on his chest. "I don't want another cookie."

"But—"

He bent his head and brushed his lips over hers, kissing the protest from her lips. "I don't want to eat, I don't want to talk, I don't want to think. All I want to do is make love to you until you're too exhausted to think about eating or talking or thinking...."

"Joel—"

"There's a rule I really must teach you, teacher. Silence is golden." He covered her mouth with his, and the golden silence mingled with the cool dark, until the only sound to be heard was the brush of clothes falling away from skin and the sighing of the pines in the forest.

"THIS IS HIJACKING," she protested as the firm hand on her back propelled her.

"Sweetheart, you're not an airplane. This isn't a hijacking, it's a kidnapping."

Alison hadn't seen Joel all day. He'd been absent from her class; he hadn't been absent from her heart. And then in the late afternoon, when she'd trudged up the steps to her porch, hot, exhausted and worried about him, wondering where he was and what he was thinking, she'd found him standing cool and complacent in her cabin. Dressed in his usual brief attire of swim trunks and sweatshirt, he'd held her packed duffel bag in his capable hands, the gleam in his brown eyes as sexy as sin. Now he was capably pushing her out the door.

"Joel, wherever we're going can wait long enough for me to take a shower."

Her protest was halfhearted, and he seemed to know it. He paid not a whit of attention to her, just kept on guiding her out the door, down the steps and along the rise toward the lake, his arm around her waist casual yet determined.

She was afraid to believe he was really walking along beside her, taking the initiative, literally kidnapping her. She was afraid to believe what her heart wanted to believe, that he wanted to be with her, needed to be with her, as badly as she wanted and needed to be with him. "If this is a ritual drowning, I'd just as soon not participate."

"Ritual drowning?" He stopped short and turned to face her, one eyebrow climbing. It was the first time he'd looked directly into her eyes. "For a scientific type, your mind has strange little nooks and crannies." He stared down at her, and she held her breath. The look in his eyes was possessive, intimate, sensual. The excitement inside her refused to be contained. It bubbled up, spilled over, warmed her skin, brightened her eyes. Could he feel the restless flaring of her senses, see the warmth in her cheeks? Perhaps he could, for he said, "And I want to explore every one of those nooks and crannies." He raised his hand and brushed a knuckle down her cheek. "In private. Away from the madding crowd. Will you come with me, Alison?"

His look, his touch, the admission of his need to be with her—any one of those alone would have been enough to make her agree to follow him to the ends of the earth. Sexual excitement blossomed deeply in her, making her forget the long day she'd had and the worrying she'd done about him. He was here beside her, and he was asking her to go with him. Her world was complete. Yet a sixth sense told her not to reveal too much of her delight. A vulnerable, out-on-the-limb Joel, a Joel in full pursuit, was a rare wonder that must be treated with care. "Am I allowed to ask where we're going?"

"After a day of telling every kid in sight exactly what to do, I would think you'd be glad to hand the reins of responsibility to me." His knuckle nudged her cheek in gentle punishment.

"I am. It's just that I don't quite know . . . what you want from me."

She hadn't meant the words to be provocative. She'd meant them to be honest. Had she thought his eyes were sinful? They turned positively wicked. "When the time is right, woman, I will make it graphically clear what I want from you. For now you are required only to follow along, docile and smiling, pretending you've never heard of the twentieth century and feminism." He cupped her face in his hands and gazed down at her, a new and tender light in his eyes. "I think I'm asking you to trust me." A beat of silence went by while she stood caught in the deep beauty of his eyes fixed on hers. "Maybe if you trust me, I can learn to trust myself."

She moved to grasp his shoulders, wanting very badly to melt into his arms. "Joel—"

A shout from the campsite made his eyes shift. He smiled ruefully. "Don't look at me like that, sweet. Not . . . yet."

The mood broken, he grasped her hand and turned to lead her to the shoreline, where a sailboat was beached. Rigged and ready, the little boat's blue fiberglass hull shone with polishing, the sail swinging in a lazy arc over it. The well was big enough for her duffel bag as well as the large one already stowed inside. Joel reached in, dragged out two life belts, snapped one under her breasts with averted eyes and a brisk, impersonal touch, then put on the other.

Sitting inside the boat as it skimmed over the lake, her knees at a right angle to Joel's, Alison felt the breeze lifting and freeing her hair. Something else tugged loose and floated free: her worries about Joel. They melted away in the blaze of sunshine, in the late-afternoon deep blue of the sky, in the shush of water against the hull. Or was it the sight of Joel that sent her worries flying to the four winds? Seated with one buttock balanced on the broad flare of fiberglass and one lean hand curled around the tiller, the other grasping the rope that controlled the angle of the sail, he looked pleased with himself, supremely masculine, as satisfied as a pirate who'd just boarded a prize ship.

She tore her eyes away from him and turned to look at a seagull wheeling lazily in the sky. Etched against the blue, the white bird was all that was graceful, an artist's sculpture in motion.

Behind her Joel murmured, "Jonathan Livingston Seagull." Her eyes dropped to his; his turned mischievous. "I presume?" An eyebrow lifted, and the accent was subtly British.

So quick and perceptive was his associating the famous bird who strove for perfection with David Livingstone, the African explorer, that Alison laughed. Joel grinned back at her, and she was struck by an acute sense of intimacy. She said, "You have some strange little nooks and crannies of your own."

He beamed a thousand-volt smile at her. "And are you going to explore every one?"

With one hand on the tiller and the other on the sheet, he was essentially defenseless. She put a hand out in a playful, halfhearted attempt to push him overboard. She didn't budge him an inch. A solid wall of unresisting muscle met the palm of her hand.

The course of his small ship as steady as ever, he said slowly, "Assault on the captain's body by a crew member is a mutinous act, punishable by whatever sentence the captain decrees fitting."

But entranced by the feel of warm, hair-sprinkled skin under her hand, she laid her other palm on his chest, directly over his nipple. "What kind of punishment does the captain think fits the crime?" She raised blue, flirtatious eyes to his face.

"Normally we strap the hapless sailor to the mizzenmast and let him have a taste of the cat-o'-nine-tails on his back. In your case, however, a different punishment might be called for."

With a skill and daring she didn't know she had, she let her hands drift lower. "The captain has other ideas for me?" Her hands were at his waist, lingering, drifting. . . .

His eyes narrowed. "Something suitable will be arranged. Perhaps . . . confinement. Long-term. In the same bed with the captain." Her hands moved lower. His hand on the sail jerked; the boat's hull banged against a wave that was hit at the wrong angle. "Behave yourself, Alison, or we'll capsize." He tossed both accent and act away in his efforts to correct the boat's course.

A smile on her lips, she obeyed instantly and sat back, balancing on the edge of the boat. Turning her head, she gazed into the blueness of the sky, thinking that his admission of vulnerability made her want to soar like that bird. . . .

"Now what are you doing?"

The husky words sounded velvet rough.

"I'm behaving myself." Surprised at his question, she turned to look at him and found his heated eyes traveling over her.

"Who told you to do that?"

"The captain."

"What does he know?"

He wanted her to touch him again, and he was telling her so with his mouth, with his eyes.

A motorboat with a water-skier behind whizzed by them, rocking them in its wake and forcing Joel to turn the boat into the undulating waves. "The captain doesn't know enough to pay attention to what he's doing, obviously." He struggled to keep the boat turned into the churning water to minimize the rocking. "Don't think you're going to escape scot-free, my sweet."

She didn't. When Joel beached the sailboat on a deserted island of sand and rock and scrub pine, he told her part of her punishment would be to find kindling wood. He sent her to clamor over the rocky, sandy interior of the island while he pitched a small tent under the shade of the tallest pine. When she returned with a bundle of sticks under her arm, what she had already guessed had become a reality. Joel meant to spend the night on this bit of earth rising from the lake. The small orange tent sat shiny and secure under the protective branches, and Joel had already built a fire pit of stone a safe way from the entrance and the surrounding trees.

When he saw her, he rose from his work and came to take the bundle from under her arm. In his eyes was the unspoken question: *is this all right, are you pleased?*

She handed him the twigs she'd gathered, her answer written in her eyes and the movements of her body.

As if the sudden intimacy disturbed him, he turned away from her and laid the crackling wood inside the circle of stones. When he rose, his eyes were sober. "Shall we swim before supper or afterward?"

His guarded look made Alison cautious. The intimacy was gone, vanished, even as the night softened and the crickets chirped, enclosing them in a cocoon. She thought about how much she wanted to plunge into the cool water and feel his legs tangling with hers. But the look in his eyes made her say, "Perhaps we should eat first."

They went about their tasks easily, yet carefully avoided touching or looking at each other. Squatting in front of the fire, Joel brought an astounding array of snacks out of his bag, cocktail wieners to roast on sticks, potato and banana chips and his own concoction of energy food, a combination of coconut, chocolate bits, mixed nuts, granola and wheat germ. There were marshmallows for dessert and a sweet-tart white wine to drink.

They started by roasting the wieners on long, thin branches, and then began the serious business of eating, using their fingers. When Alison had taken the edge off her hunger and drunk a substantial amount of the wine out of a paper cup, she chased a cocktail wiener with a banana chip and made a face.

"Strange, confusing combination. I'm not sure if I should make cocktail-party conversation or go find a tree to climb."

"Are you belittling my cuisine, woman?"

"Not belittling it exactly, just trying to bring my mind and my stomach into harmony. Each one thinks the other has gone berserk."

She leaned over to lay her roasting stick to one side and accidentally caught the edge of his as he held it over the fire, making the wiener he was roasting jiggle off the end and fall into the flames. Startled, she stared, watching the bit of meat turn black, a chuckle bubbling up from her throat.

"What heartless wench is this that I have on me hands? She takes the food from a starving man's mouth and then laughs—"

"Starving? You've had eleven of those things."

He raised an eyebrow and said in a mock cynical tone, "But who's counting?"

Glad he'd dropped his careful casualness and his silence, she pressed on. "You've had so many of those things I thought you'd start to oink by now."

Slowly, carefully, he got to his feet. "I *will* have retribution, woman."

Bracing herself on her palms behind her, she flung her head back to look at him. "Do your worst, Captain Bligh. I'll not take back a thing I've said." For a long, endless moment, he stood looking down at her. She knew full well she'd goaded him, but she didn't care. The next move was his.

He made it so quickly, scooping and lifting her into his arms before she realized he'd moved. She had no time to cry out and scarcely none to breathe. His expression purposeful, he turned toward the lake. "You did say you'd missed your shower, didn't you?"

"Joel, don't. I don't have extra clothes—"

"Yes, you do." His cool, no-nonsense voice was meant to strike terror in her heart, and it nearly did. "I packed them for you."

"Joel, I . . . *Joel!*"

He walked straight into the water with her.

The icy wet splashing against skin not warmed by his arms and chest sent shivers dancing over her. She turned her face into him, clinging to his shoulders in a desperate, ridiculous attempt to stay dry. Her bottom connected with the water; moisture pooled over her stomach. Shorts and shirt turned soggy and stuck to her body. Her hair dragged down her back with the wetness.

When he was chest-deep in the water and she expected to be thrown away from him in one glorious, retributive toss, she found he had no such intention. He let her legs slip down until her body floated next to his. He stood securely on the lake bottom; she remained above water by the simple expedient of winding her arms around his neck. "Joel, I'm in over my head."

"So am I," he said huskily, wrapping his arms around her waist and bringing her body to that exquisite fit against his, letting her feel his need for her. "So am I."

"What are you going to do about it?"

"Drown myself . . . in you."

He carried her back to the tent, stripped her of her wet clothes, took off his own and made love to her with a tender, desperate need. He was that most fragile of all things on earth, a man aware of his own vulnerability. She tried to show him with her mouth and hands that she understood, that she was hungry, that she needed him desperately, too.

Later, when they lay side by side, Joel said huskily, "I'm not sleepy. I think I'll go out by the fire."

"I'll come with you."

In the silence she held her breath, waiting for his reply. The quiet went on for an eternity.

"There's a sweatshirt and pants inside your bag," he said at last. "Wear them. I don't want you getting chilled."

He had the fire blazing when she emerged. He'd gotten more wood, she saw from the pile stacked outside the rocks. How long did he intend to stay up?

He was seated on the ground, a sweater bunched under his rear, his gaze on the fire. She sat down beside him and let her head drift to his shoulder. He muttered something and pulled her head down to rest in the sheltered curve of his thigh and abdomen. "You're tired. You should have stayed inside."

Her head comfortably in his lap, her legs stretched out, she tilted her head to watch the play of firelight and shadow on his face. "I wanted to be with you."

He stared at her for a moment, then reached for the wiener stick he'd placed close at hand. She heard the rustle of a bag, watched as he threaded a marshmallow on the pointed tip. When he leaned forward to hold the stick over the fire, the edge of his open jacket brushed her cheek. The smell of the burning sweet joined the smokier scent of the fire. While she watched, he eased the toasty morsel off the stick and held it to her lips. She took it into her mouth, loving him with her eyes. He said, "You almost make me believe this is the real world." The fire danced on his cheeks, darkened his eyes, shadowed his jaw.

Her heart accelerating, she lifted her hand to his nape. "This world is as real as you want it to be."

"Alison—"

"Kiss me, Joel. Just kiss me."

He tasted marshmallow; he tasted her. And discovered he was too hungry for just a taste.

8

"ARE THOSE DARK CIRCLES under your eyes cause for celebration or commiseration?" Eve Cunningham lifted the mug of wine in Alison's direction and settled more deeply into the flowery chair.

Alison's smile was rueful. She should have known Eve would read the signs and guess that she and Joel had become lovers. "I'm not sure."

Eve waited, but when Alison didn't say more, she shrugged. "To what do I owe the rare and unexpected pleasure of an evening of your company?"

Alison flushed. "I have been neglecting you, haven't I?"

"Actually, I've been neglecting you. Benign neglect, as they say. I did drop in for a few minutes that day you held class in the cafeteria, but you were too busy to notice."

"Did you think you'd stepped into the middle of World War Three?"

"I thought I was watching one of the most successful classes I've ever seen in my long years of riding herd on this camp."

"Thank you." Pleased that Eve had understood what she'd been trying to do and that she approved, Alison sipped her rosé. The sweet-tart taste lingered in her mouth, made her remember how Joel had fed her that toasted marshmallow and had shared the taste with her. . . .

"So. That's out of the way. Have you thought any more about returning next year?"

"I'm not sure I want to commit myself to another summer until I know what I'm going to be doing this fall." Alison's eyes met Eve's.

"So Joel hasn't come to his senses yet."

Alison put down her mug and walked to the window to stare out into the twilight. June had become July almost while she wasn't looking. The fireflies had dwindled to an occasional single flare lighting the shadows. The croak of frogs had been replaced by the quack of mallard ducks and the haunting cry of the loon. "Maybe he has. Maybe I'm the one who's crazy."

"No, Alison. You're not the one who's crazy." There was a click of pottery against wood, and then Eve came to stand behind her, her arm going around Alison's shoulders. "From what I've seen of Joel, he's worth any effort it takes to make him see what he has in you."

"I've tried almost everything. There's not much left."

"Try loving him without worrying about the future or thinking about your pride. He'll come around."

Alison turned to the older woman and saw the love and concern in her face. "I wish I could be as sure of that as you are."

Eve smiled. "We antediluvian types have been around for a long time. We've seen it all. It's hard to fool us. You'll find a way to make him see the truth, Alison, I know you will."

YOU'LL FIND A WAY.

Easy for you to say, Eve Cunningham. Alison cut

through the cool lake, eating up the distance with a slow, steady crawl. It was Friday afternoon, and she'd come out to the glistening blue water to exercise away her nervous tension. Her stint at the camp was nearly at an end. Only one more day, and that was to be an activity day that Eve was planning for the students and all the parents who were able to attend. Eve had shown Alison the schedule. Races, swimming and sailing and a camp fire in the evening were planned.

Since that morning Alison had been struggling not to give in to a blue mood. Joel hadn't come to her last night, though she'd waited with the light on in her cabin till well past the hour when he was finished at the club.

One missed night did not the end of an affair make, she thought, paraphrasing Diana's sage words. Everyone was so willing to give advice, Diana preaching caution, Eve faith. She hadn't followed Eve's counsel about swallowing her pride, either. Pride was a lonely bedfellow; she knew that now firsthand. When she'd finally accepted that Joel wasn't coming and had turned off the light, she'd lain in the darkness with her eyes wide open, not even caring that sleep was elusive. The bed had been too big and empty to be comfortable.

So what was she going to do? Her arms turned leaden, but she went on swimming.

She had a scientific mind, but this wasn't a problem that would yield a solution through logical thinking. Joel was not a scientific equation. One plus one did not equal two where he was concerned. Since the night he'd kidnapped her, she was almost certain he cared for her. She had tried to show him how much she cared for him without actually telling him she loved him. She knew him well enough to realize that those were words he didn't want to hear. But beyond hitting the man over the head with a blunt instrument and dragging him away, cave-woman style, she simply didn't know what else she could do.

He was intractable, immovable and impossibly stubborn, but he was also captivating, charming and impossibly sexy. And worth every minute of her agonizing over him if there was the slightest chance he might change his mind and decide to spend his life with her. After their night on the island, she'd had such hopes. And such dreams.

Alison turned back toward the dock, knowing she'd swum long enough, knowing, too, that she was no closer to solving the problem of Joel than she had been when she dived into the water.

Back at the cabin, she took a hot shower and toweled herself dry. Dressed in her denim pants and a warm sweater, she settled down to read the letter from Diana that had been waiting for her when she'd returned from her swim.

So how is my scientific sister doing in the wilds of the Adirondacks? All I know about them is that they belong to the Appalachian chain and that the Appalachians are old, worn-down mountains and the Rocky Mountains are young, rugged mountains. That is the sum total of what I learned in geography class. Can you use it in any of yours?

Things are fine here. You're lucky you missed out on the haying. The baler broke down, and Dad broke a tooth biting his tongue to keep from saying what he wanted to say because I was sitting there on the tractor listening. Unfortunately, he got it fixed—the baler, not his tooth; he has to wait two weeks for an appointment with the dentist— and I had to help him finish up the hay. Are you coming home Sunday or not? Dad asked me, and I lied and told him I didn't know for sure. Then I realized I really didn't know for sure. You do have a return ticket for Sunday, don't you? You haven't said you were coming home then. Has something happened to change your plans? If you want us to meet the plane, you'll have to give us a call the night before. You know how long it takes to get to Des Moines from the boondocks where we live.

Your friend David called and wanted to know when you were coming home. How *can* you encourage that creep? He's so thin he makes a scarecrow look tasty. You were certainly reticent—I love that word, but every time I use it I have to look up the spelling—about your trip to New York City. Did you see the luscious Joel Brandon or didn't you?

Guilt washed over Alison in waves. In her letters home, she hadn't mentioned Joel's presence in the mountains. Her sister would have asked too many questions that Alison couldn't have answered.

I am, of course, dying of curiosity. Which keeps me alive, because I'm also dying of boredom. I'm thinking of getting a job with a construction firm next summer rather than coming home to the farm to vegetate. Do I have your blessing? I know you think we have an obligation to help Dad summers, since he got stuck with two females and no sons, but honestly, Alison, I feel as if I'm going to die. Come home soon and at least keep me company. We can be bored together.

P.S. Are there any good-looking men in them thar hills? As you may remember, I prefer them young and rugged, not old and worn down.

A smile on her lips, Alison laid down the letter. It was already too late to send an answer. She would arrive home before the letter would.

If she went home. In the gathering twilight, she stared into the emptiness of the room and wished she knew what to do.

In that same hazy twilight a few miles away, Joel stood in the chest-high chilly water at Fish Creek Beach. Six feet away Marty bobbed, grinning at him.

"Okay, ace. You can tread water. Now let's see your Olympic style." Joel had to admit that either Marty was an apt pupil or he himself had hidden talents as a teacher. In four sessions the boy had become a passable swimmer. In the waist-deep water, Marty swam furiously toward Joel, legs churning, head coming up in rhythm with his right arm. He was still stroking too fast, but Joel assured him he would be able to slow his pace with a little more practice.

During this last time together, Joel added a refinement. At Marty's age he'd been caught by the street bully and thrown into a pool. Even though he'd known how to swim, he'd nearly drowned because he hadn't had time to prepare himself and take a breath.

So when Joel saw that Marty could swim quite well, he explained what had happened to him. Marty's eyes snapped with anger, and Joel was touched by his loyalty. Telling Marty exactly what he planned to do, Joel hoisted the boy to stand on his shoulders and told him to get ready.

The first few times, Joel let Marty give the signal when he was ready to be jettisoned headfirst into the water. But as Marty gained confidence, Joel took the initiative, so that the boy never knew for sure when he would be dumped into the lake.

It developed into a game that Marty wanted to play endlessly. When the darkness had set in and the cold had them both shivering, Joel finally threw his arm around Marty's shoulders, and they sloshed through the shallow water onto the sand to drop, exhausted, onto their towels.

With energy to burn, Marty mopped his dripping hair and then sat up on a propped elbow to look at Joel. "I had a great time. You were super."

"Maybe super, but not Superman. I've found muscles that are so old I must have had them in mothballs."

The boy grinned at the man, admiration and affection pouring from every freckle. "A hot shower and you'll be good as new."

"Thanks. Let me talk to you again in a few years and see how you feel about straining your older, more mature body with excessive exercise."

Marty flushed, clasped his hands around his knees and sat up to look out over the dusky sand. "I should

be in as good shape as I am now. If I keep on dancing."
His eyes dropped, and he picked up a handful of sand
and let it fall through his fingers.

"You're a dancer?"

"Yeah." He made a face, and the happiness that had
been there a moment ago drained away. With a sardonic twist of his lips, he said, "You know, all wimps
are dancers."

"Tell that to Rudolf Nureyev or Gregory Hines or
Gene Kelly."

"Yeah, sure. They're big stars. They don't have to go
to school in Syracuse and get mocked out."

Joel's eyes met Marty's. "Somewhere, sometime in
their lives, they got mocked out. Have you heard that
old line some Hollywood exec cracked about Fred As-
taire? 'Can't sing, can't act, can dance a little.' Anybody who sets himself a high goal gets ridiculed."

"You got mocked out?"

"Every day, buddy."

"But you kept going."

"It was that or listen to the voice inside my head
mocking me out because I wasn't doing what I wanted
to do."

"Mom wants me to be something sensible like a
doctor or a lawyer or work in virus research." He pulled
a face. "That's what Ken—*nith* does."

"Who's Kenneth, your stepfather?"

Marty nodded.

"Do you ever see your other dad?"

"Once in a while. He's not too interested in me. He's
got his own career." He said the words coolly and with
a shrug of his shoulders, as if he'd accepted the situa-

tion philosophically. "I suppose I shouldn't knock him. He does put out a bundle for my dancing lessons."

Joel felt a fleeting distaste for the man who could treat with such carelessness this sensitive, intelligent boy who was starved for male companionship, but he carefully kept the sympathy from his voice and face. "Are you any good?"

Marty sat very still, his mouth tightening in indecision. Then he sprang to his feet, executed a neat leap and brought his heels together. He ended the impromptu step by coming down in a perfect split on the soft sand. His agility and coordination equaled that of the professional dancers Joel had seen on the stage.

"I guess you are. No wonder you learned to swim so quickly. Your body is used to doing what you tell it to do."

"Yeah, I've got good coordination. It's in my genes, I guess, a gift from the old man. One of the few he ever gave me."

"It is a gift, one you can accept or toss away. So what are you going to do with it?"

Marty drew the towel around his shoulders. "It's hard going against my mother all the time."

"Maybe you're giving her conflicting signals. My guess is when you make up your mind you're going to be the best dancer you can be, she'll go along." Joel smiled. "I seem to remember that after Leonard Bernstein became famous, someone chided his father for trying to dissuade his son in his early years from going into music. The father answered, 'How did I know he was going to be Leonard Bernstein?' We have to define who we are, not let other people tell us what we should do and who we should be."

Marty squinted at Joel. "That's what you did, huh?"

"That's what I did." Joel picked up his towel and took Marty's hand to tug him to his feet. "Nobody's perfect. I'm still working on it, ace."

When they returned to the car, Marty was silent as he pulled on a warm sweatshirt and stuck his sandy feet into his jeans. Joel let the silence continue, knowing Marty needed the quiet to think.

At the campsite, the boy got out of the car reluctantly. He put his hand on the car window, just as he'd done that first time Joel brought him home, and his chin tilted at a stubborn angle. This time, it was obvious Marty was fighting to hide his regret that their hours together were over. Joel's own throat felt tight. He'd come to like Marty more than he would have thought possible.

"Will I ever see you again after I leave tomorrow?"

"Do you want to see me again?" asked Joel.

Marty nodded. Joel suspected the boy would have had trouble making his vocal chords work at that moment.

"Then you'll see me again. How are you at writing letters?"

"Lousy."

"Practice up. I'll give you my address."

Marty grinned suddenly. "And your telephone number?"

Joel gave the boy a lopsided smile of his own, along with his business card. "And my telephone number. As long as you promise not to call me before one o'clock in the afternoon."

"I promise."

Joel sketched a salute and put the car in gear.

"Joel?"

"Yes."

"Thanks . . . for everything."

Joel smiled. "You're welcome."

"Listen I . . . uh, hope things work out with you and the teach."

"Thanks, kid. I think you've got good taste in women, too."

The boy flushed. "Kathryn's okay. See you tomorrow?"

Joel hesitated. "I'm not sure. I'm working on some new material, and I need some time to see how it will go."

Marty forgot to look tough and looked forlorn instead. "So long, Joel."

"So long, kid. See you on Broadway."

Marty summoned up a smile. "Sure. See you on Broadway."

AT TEN MINUTES AFTER MIDNIGHT, Alison walked into the Pine Tree Lounge. Joel hardly recognized her. She was wearing a floaty dress of sheer yellow material that was kept modest by the matching slip underneath. Her hair was pinned up at the sides in a sophisticated style that made her look citified and lovely. Not that she wasn't lovely with it down. He preferred to see her hair down, especially spread over his pillow. . . .

Dangerous thoughts those. He dragged his mind away from them, but he couldn't take his eyes off her. She looked like spring walking into that dark lounge, and he felt his stomach clench as if he'd been given a one-two punch by a champion boxer.

He was in the middle of his monologue. Unfortunately for him, it was new material, copy that he'd written since he'd come to the mountains. Marty had partially inspired it; his own teenage years had supplied the rest.

He went on with his act, a portion of his mind juggling the mental pictures he used as memory aids, the other portion watching Alison. She went to the bar and ordered a drink. Then she turned casually, one hip on a bar stool, to watch him perform. Her back was ramrod straight. He remembered kissing that lovely back all the way down to the sweet hollow....

How cool she looked in that pale yellow. Her face was just as cool. Joel didn't know why she'd come. He only knew it gave him both pleasure and pain to see her.

He resisted the temptation to cut his monologue short and decided to play out the full twenty minutes of material that now seemed too self-revealing. The bartender offered her her drink. Alison took it and rose to walk gracefully to a table against the wall, settling into a chair that provided her with a full view of him.

The room seemed suddenly warmer by ten degrees. He could feel perspiration gathering under the collar of his shirt and sliding down his back. Too bad he didn't have her talent for looking and staying cool.

Alison rubbed her fingers on the side of the dewy glass that held her piña colada and knew she was listening to a master. Joel was working his usual magic on the crowd and making his delivery look effortless. He gave no indication that he'd noticed her entrance, but he had to have seen her.

She shouldn't have come. She felt conspicuous in her summery dress; every other woman in the place was in shorts or jeans. But none of them was engaged in battle strategy as elaborate as hers.

There was just one small problem. Now that she was here she didn't know what she would do if Joel simply nodded to her and walked out the door. She sipped her drink and tried to hold her shaking knees together, wishing desperately she had stayed home in her cabin.

He was finishing up his monologue. He told the audience good-night and stepped down from the tiny, raised area in the corner that served as a stage. She tried a smile and hoped it didn't look as shaky as she felt.

At her table, he stopped. "Hello, Joel."

He dipped his head. "Hello, sweet. Aren't you out a little late for a working lady?"

"Some of us are out late, some of us work late." He bowed again, acknowledging the truth of her words. When he raised his head, his eyes gleamed with amusement. Encouraged, she said, "May I buy you a drink?"

"I'm sorry, no. I've been advised to watch my alcoholic intake by a young woman who's worried about my nutrition."

She no longer had to work to make her smile genuine. "Smart lady."

"Who doesn't seem to practice what she teaches." He eyed the elaborate curved glass in front of her. "Did you order your drink to match your dress?"

"As a matter of fact I did. I have it on the best authority that the comedian appearing here only goes home with the women who color coordinate their drinks with their clothes." She didn't know where the outrageous words had come from. She only knew that everything about him was challenging her and that she would never win unless she went into the fray with all flags flying.

"As I've said before, you're an amazing font of information." With that noncommittal answer, he slid into the chair opposite her and lifted his hand to indicate he wanted service. A drink was brought, obviously his usual. He didn't touch it.

"You decided to have a drink, after all?"

"The house provides me with sustenance. There was no need for you to pay."

She eyed the burgundy liquid in the glass and then the dark-green unstructured jacket he wore. "You forgot to color coordinate."

A smile tugged at his lips. "I'll go home with the comedian no matter what I drink."

Her eyes lifted to his, but nothing of what he was thinking was in his face. "I'd like to be able to say that." Leaving him to deal with that rapier-sharp bit of honesty, she sidestepped the issue. "You weren't in class today." She rushed on, not wanting him to think she needed to know where he'd been and what he'd been doing. This was hard, harder than she'd thought it would be, and she was getting no cooperation from him. "The kids missed you. They asked about you." That brought no response from him, either. She looked down at her glass, drew a pattern in the dewy moisture on the side. Eve was wrong. She shouldn't have swallowed her pride. She should have stayed in her cabin and done twenty more sit-ups. Still eyeing her glass, she said, "I'd like, just once, to know what you're thinking."

She looked up at him then. His expression didn't change, yet there was a flare of interest and admiration in his eyes that gave her hope.

"I was thinking how out of place you look here. Almost as out of place as you looked in that club in the city."

It was so far from what she'd expected him to say that each word was like a blow. Her pride was all she had left. She lifted her chin. Her cheeks were flushed, and her eyes sparkled. "As out of place as I would look in your life?"

"An interesting analogy. And an apropos one. I would say the ratio was the same."

"Well, that's plain enough, I guess." Embarrassed warmth rushed into her cheeks. She looked down at her drink, feeling the complete fool. She wanted—needed—to escape, but she also needed a few minutes to compose herself before she got up and walked away from Joel. When she looked up and saw that he was watching her with hawklike intensity, examining her to see if his words had had the desired effect, she clenched her teeth and rose gracefully from her chair. "Since you've made everything quite clear, I'll say goodbye—"

He was on his feet, his hand on her arm before she could turn away. "I'll follow you home."

"That's not necessary."

"Not for your sake. For mine."

Outside the breeze lifted her skirt to swirl it around her legs, reminding her that her elaborate preparations had been wasted. His car was parked close to the building, hers farther out. She walked alone to hers, got in and slammed the door. She gunned the motor and raced out of the parking lot. Just because he had some misguided, chivalrous idea about seeing her safely home didn't mean she had to make it easy for him.

Filled with a wild urge to prove something—she wasn't sure quite what—Alison drove too fast along the curving road. The rental car rattled in protest, but she ignored it and pressed down on the accelerator. She went around a curve, and Joel's lights disappeared, then reappeared. She hadn't lost him.

Joel watched the red taillights whizzing around curves in front of him and thought grimly, *The little fool is going to kill herself.* Alison took another curve with reckless skill, and the nerves in his stomach tightened. She was a good driver, but if anything happened to her, it would be his fault. He shouldn't have rejected her there in a public place. He should have waited until they were alone.

But Joel knew what would have happened if he'd waited. He would have followed her home and gone inside with her, stripped that frothy dress off her body and loved her till they were both exhausted.

She went too fast around another curve. He gripped the wheel, wishing his hands were around her neck. She needed a good talking to.

Alison glanced in her rearview mirror. The man was sticking to her like a burr. Still, it hardly made sense to try to lose him. He did know where she lived. At least he wouldn't follow her into the drive that led to the camp compound, she was sure. The access to his cabin was on another road.

She was wrong. When she turned into the lane, he was right behind her. In the moonlit clearing she pulled up in front of her cabin, stopped the car and got out. Behind her, Joel slammed his door with an ominous whack and followed her up the cabin steps. At the door she turned. "As you can see, I'm safely home."

"A fact due to benevolent gods more than careful driving." He stood a foot away from her, looking annoyed, irritated and exasperated.

Fine. Good. At least she could make him feel some emotion, even if it wasn't love.

Joel had the urge to pull her close and kiss her senseless. Not a hair on that immaculate head was out of place. She looked as cool and unruffled as she had when she'd walked into the lounge. He was filled with an overwhelming urge to disturb that cool poise in any way he could.

Alison looked at his face and decided she wasn't going to ask him if she would see him tomorrow. Let him stay in his cabin and write or sleep or whatever it was he did. Let him vegetate there. "Will I see you tomorrow?"

He seemed not to hear her. "You look too beautiful to touch." He hadn't meant to say that. It had just come out, as if he couldn't contain the thought any longer.

To Alison, Joel seemed as unmoved as he had when they'd climbed the steps, yet something in his voice told her his mood had changed. Her heart lifting, she said, "Are you going to touch me?"

Every sensible, reasonable thought in his head told him the answer must be no. His feet moved, and he went to her, clasping his hands around her small waist, belted tightly in the close-fitting chiffon. Deliberately he splayed his hands over her abdomen. "Yes, God help me, I'm going to touch you." He cradled her hips in his hands and drew her closer.

Lifting her arms, Alison put her palms on his shoulders, her heart singing. She shouldn't give in to him like this so quickly. She should make him suffer a little. "I really dislike you a lot, Mr. Brandon."

"The feeling is mutual, Ms Powell. I kept thinking that if by some miracle you didn't kill yourself out there on the road, if I ever got my hands on you again, I'd strangle you."

"Are you still bent on murder?"

His fingers moved gently over her belly, sliding the chiffon against the silk, sending those first, stinging tingles of desire coursing through her. "Actually, it's the farthest thing from my mind at the moment."

"I'd like, just once, to know what you're thinking," she said in a soft echo of her words back at the club.

"You know what I'm thinking, woman."

His throaty intensity matched the caressing movements of his hands. She lifted sparkling eyes to him. "Not . . . precisely. Perhaps you'd care to show me?"

He was taking advantage of her, selfishly taking what she offered. It was wrong, so wrong. He should turn and go, leave her before he hurt her badly. "I'd like that very much, sweet."

Their exchange was a brief excursion into the delicious intimacy Alison sought, but after he'd released her and they had walked inside the cabin, after she'd turned on the lamp hanging over the table, she discovered he'd replaced his mask.

"Turn around."

The cool order disturbed her, but she stepped away from the table and did as he asked. Expertly he began unfastening the buttons that ran in a long row down her back. When they disappeared under the belt at her waist, he slid his hands around in front of her to unclasp her buckle. He took his time, acting as her servant, each brush of his fingers on her taut abdomen a promise of more delight to come. The belt fell to each side of her hips. He slackened it to allow him access to the tiny waist hook, tucked into the row of buttons at her back.

The night air traced chilly fingers down the sensitive skin on Alison's spine. Helped by Joel's hands, her dress floated to the floor and settled at her feet. The double onslaught of undiluted Adirondack air and his silence made shivers skim up her nape. Unsure of herself, unsure of him, she closed her eyes, waiting. His warm hand locked around her ankle, and he lifted one foot, then the other, untangling them from her dress. From his kneeling position at her feet, he tossed the yellow froth away. Then he captured her slip between his palms and her body and rose slowly, dragging the silk agonizingly, deliciously, over her thighs, hips and breasts, until he lifted it over her head and sent it skittering to the floor.

She couldn't turn, couldn't bear to look at him and see the expression on his face. The way he was undressing her was wonderfully tender, delightfully erotic . . . and terribly wrong. Her back to him, she whispered, "What . . . is it?"

He didn't answer. Gathering all her courage, wearing only a wisp of a bra and a brief lace concoction at her hips, she turned. "What's wrong?"

"I wasn't aware that something was wrong." His dark eyes moved over her. "It looks to me as if everything is quite right. You are . . . exquisite."

She felt exposed to him, as transparent, vulnerable and fragile as blown glass. He must see how much, how desperately, she loved him. A whispering sixth sense told her he did, and her love was making him feel as vulnerable as she, even though he still wore his green jacket, the correct shirt, the narrow tie. Was he thinking that he'd followed her here because he was powerless to do anything else, that at the tiniest crook of her finger he came running? Didn't he know that she had no power over him other than what he gave her? "Joel—" Thinking only of getting close to him, she stepped forward and glided her palms up his chest. Under her fingers, his muscles tightened as if she'd struck him. He groaned, and his arms came around her. He encircled her, pulling her so tightly to him that she could feel the imprint of his clothes on her skin. Surprised by his burst of passion, she inhaled sharply.

He was filled with a sudden, deep hatred for himself. He was pulling her close, even though he knew that pushing her away would be the best thing in the world for her. Out of his own conflicting urges, he searched desperately for a way to ensure her rejection of him.

"This is what you wanted, isn't it? Body contact? Sex?" His jacket rasped against her skin the way his words created havoc in her heart. While she was still reeling from the raw emotion in his voice, he loosened his hold on her and brushed his mouth down the side of her throat. "It better be all you want. Because it's all I have to give. It's all I've ever had to give."

"I don't believe that—"

"Then you're a fool." He pushed her away a little. "Love is a joke played on the human race by Mother Nature. Obviously she has a better sense of humor than all of us."

Alison was looking at him with that starkly hurt look that ripped at his soul. Didn't she understand what a swine he was? Didn't she understand that he couldn't stop himself from wanting her even though he didn't love her?

He released her, turned his back to her and thrust a hand through his hair. "Usually when a woman starts looking at me the way you do, I tell her thanks a lot but no thanks and goodbye. I've meant to do that with you, but I—" He faced her, his face dark and ravaged. "You have some crazy kind of hold over me. You're deep in my mind, like an unfinished routine I can't work out." He pulled at his necktie as if he was suddenly warm. "I'd expect you to be in my life a hundred years from now."

"I would be," she cried.

"Would you? I don't think so." He reached out to stroke down her throat with one knuckle. He still wanted her, ached to have her. "How much do you love me, Alison? Enough to go to bed with me, even though I can't offer you love in return?''

His tone was silky, his face smooth, his eyes dark, guarded. She felt the pulse of anger under her skin like a living thing. Pride beat there, too, but stronger than both her anger and her pride was the conviction that the answer she gave him would be the ultimate test of her love. Could she love him that unselfishly? She hesitated, knowing that after this night there would be no doubt in his mind that she loved him. She was giving her heart into his hands, completely, without reservation and without any hope of ever being given his in return.

"I love you enough . . . to take whatever part of yourself you can give me.'' Before he could refuse her, or push her away again, she slid her hands under his jacket, pushing it down his arms and off. She unfastened his tie, unbuttoned his shirt. His eyes blazed with pleasure at being undressed by her. When he was wearing as little as she, he caught her hands and took the initiative, finishing the task of undressing her as if he was unwrapping a priceless present. Then he carried her to the bed.

His lovemaking was passionate, demanding, all consuming. She gave and gave, murmuring the love words that had been denied her before. He kissed them from her mouth, but the moment he lifted his lips to explore the silken skin of her breasts, she told him again how beautiful he was and how much she adored him.

Each murmured word drove him to new heights of sensual expertise. And when at last he made her his, there was nothing left for her to say. She was beyond words, beyond thought. All that was left was Joel, Joel, Joel....

9

WHEN SHE AWOKE in the morning, he was gone.

In the bed she had shared with him, she turned her face into the pillow and moaned in distress. She had gambled and lost.

Had she expected that morning to start differently? Had she thought he would be there to kiss her awake, to tell her that he loved her? She'd been wrong, so wrong.

How was it possible to know a man so well, to lie in his arms and receive his kisses and caresses and still not understand him? How was it possible to possess and be possessed and yet remain alone?

His lovemaking had been passionate, possessive, soul destroying. Nerves, muscles, bones vibrated with the memory of his touch and the aching longing to have him there beside her.

Alison crawled out of bed and stepped into her shower, hoping the hot water would bring her awake. But perversely, as the water pulsed over her, she wanted, needed, blessed oblivion.

The solace of a blank mind eluded her. She remembered, remembered....

After a careful application of makeup and a cup of black coffee, she tugged on a bright yellow sleeveless sweatshirt and denim shorts and felt nearly ready to face the day. She came out of her cabin and walked down the steps, crossing the clearing to the dining hall, where Eve waited for her. There was a freshness in the air, a brilliance in the sky. Clouds floated near the treed peaks of the mountains, fluffy white puffs that threatened nothing more serious than an occasional, fleeting shadow over the ground. Everything—the pines, the land, the sky—filled her senses with their beauty, yet the intense joy she might have felt on such a day was denied her. She was too filled with bittersweet longing.

In the dining hall, Eve took one look at her. Her shrewd eyes saw past the makeup applied to hide the dark circles, the carefully arranged smile. "Are you sure you're up to this?"

Alison's camouflage had failed her. "I'm fine." She averted her eyes and picked up a stack of gunnysacks lying inside a cardboard box, transferring them to the table. Eve had already removed a mind-boggling collection from several cardboard boxes and spread it over three tables. Rainbow-colored balls, Hula Hoops, flags, ribbons, baseball bats, badminton birdies and other assorted pieces of game equipment were scattered in various piles, organized chaos.

"Here," Eve said, dropping a whistle strung on a loop of red yarn over Alison's head. "You'll need this. Guard it with your life. It's the only thing that will keep you sane." Eve's green eyes sought, found hers. "And keep your chin up. The game isn't over yet."

The expression in her eyes told Alison she wasn't talking about the games at camp. "Yes," she said, "it is."

"Well." Eve's eyes dropped. "I'm sorry to hear that."

Alison's smile was wry. "I'm sorry to say it."

"Never an ill wind. If you aren't getting married—" the words sent a shock of pain through Alison "—then you'll be coming back next summer."

She shook her head. "I couldn't."

"I see." Eve took her refusal calmly, as if she'd expected it. "Unfortunate. You showed definite promise." Eve gave her a reluctant smile. "I'll miss you."

"I'll miss you, too, Eve. You've been a good friend."

Eve shrugged off the sober words. "You might not think so when you get to the end of this day. I've lost more repeat possibilities for teacher candidates after Activity Day. That's why I thought I'd get you to commit yourself this morning." She smiled a self-effacing smile. "The joke's on me. Well. Let me tell you where to take this stuff. The gunnysacks go to that grassy place in front of the hall, and the Hula Hoops go down by the dock, and the badminton court has to be set up over by your cabin—" Eve rapped out instructions like a general briefing her troops.

With all there was to do, Alison was able to achieve a numbness of mind that allowed her to function. By the time the first children arrived, she was perspiring from exertion and more than ready for the day to begin. For the sooner it began, the sooner it would be over.

Very quickly she saw that Eve was one-hundred-percent correct about the whistle. It was the only thing that saved her sanity. It couldn't, however, save her from Mrs. Brisdale, Marty's mother.

The woman had the bad manners to come early, Marty in tow. The boy, smart lad that he was, disappeared. Alison was trying, unsuccessfully, to start the gunnysack race for the seven-year-olds. She had made the mistake of handing out the sacks without giving the youngsters strict orders to stand still. She had instantly created ten Mexican jumping beans over which she hadn't the slightest control. On top of which Mrs. Brisdale—"Call me Heather, dear, please do"—considered it her official duty to chat with Alison.

"Marty has told us so much about you I really feel you're a friend you've done such a wonderful job with him he's never been so interested in science before—"

Betsy's blond head disappeared completely inside her sack. She brought her hands up to close the opening and locked it over her head, saying she was pretending to be the garbage. Terry got tangled in the folds of his and tumbled headfirst onto the grass beside Betsy.

"And it was your friend Mr. Brandon who taught Marty to swim Kenneth thinks it's just wonderful what that young man has done with our boy he is a bit difficult you know—"

Jordan and Lisa were taking practice jumps on the same six inches of turf. Jordan bumped into Lisa and knocked her down, giving her a bloody nose. Lisa wailed like a banshee. Alison rushed over to pick her up and stanch the flow with a tissue, all the while praying that an ambulance crew on twenty-four-hour alert was close at hand.

"Oh, dear, she seems to have hurt herself is there anything I can do should someone be called—"

Lisa's mother appeared out of nowhere and, like a ministering angel, gathered up Lisa with calm expediency, told Alison not to worry, that Lisa seemed to get nosebleeds frequently. The doctor had said it was nothing to worry about, and would Alison direct her someplace where she could get some ice to put on her little girl's nose?

Grateful for one voice of sanity in this outdoor madhouse, Alison directed her to the dining hall and told her about the coolerful of ice and soda pop that sat behind the serving bar.

Lisa's mother towed the child away, while Lisa clutched the tissue to her nose and wailed her protest at being disqualified from the race and the injustice of being put out of commission by a person of the male gender.

Alison breathed a sigh of relief, only to turn and discover that her gunnysack contestants were scattered across the lawn like grazing sheep. And Mrs. Brisdale had materialized again, at her elbow.

"I do hope the little girl isn't hurt children are such a worry are you sure there isn't something I can do?"

Alison looked the woman straight in the eye. "Yes, there is something you can do. You can stand back, because I'm going to blow this whistle and I don't want to cause any damage to your eardrums."

Mrs. Brisdale's eyes widened, and she took a quick step backward. "Yes, of course," she said, the first sensible words that had come out of her mouth since she'd put her Gucci-shod feet on the campground grass. "Thank you for the warning."

An earsplitting whistle blast and a sharp order from Alison to line up did the trick. In less time than she would have thought possible, her contestants were wobbling behind the starting line, which was Terry's signal to turn and stare at Alison and say plaintively, "You can't start yet, I have to go to the bathroom."

At that precise moment, Joel sauntered down the hill.

"The day is complete," Alison muttered under her breath. "Terry, take off your sack, go to the dining hall and go to the bathroom. When you come back we'll have a special race between you and the winner. Everyone else get ready and *stand still!*"

Terry pouted and refused to move. Joel came up behind him, scooped him off his feet, threw him over his shoulder, sack and all, and headed back up the hill with him. Alison caught a fleeting glimpse of the boy's wide, surprised eyes peeping over Joel's shoulder as he jounced away.

At lunchtime she was slapping hamburgers on a grill and dealing them into buns. Being in the realm of spattering grease kept her blessedly free from Mrs. Brisdale's Liz Claiborne-suited body and her omnipresence. One o'clock rolled around, and it was time to brace herself for the competition games among her older students. After considering the possible ramifications of badminton matches, a softball tournament and a pie-eating contest, Alison decided that Eve must have an inborn sadomasochistic streak. Otherwise she would never have purposely planned this midsummer madness.

The trouble started during the badminton match. Playoff matches had eliminated all contenders except Marty and Tom.

Alison didn't like the way the two boys faced off on each side of the net. She was glad badminton required each boy to stay in his own court.

At first it looked as if they were evenly matched, with Marty having a slight edge. But as the game progressed, it was clear to Alison that Marty had been toying with his opponent. He was quick, sleek, graceful. Halfway through the match, he tired of sending Tom running from one side of the court to the other and pressed his advantage by slamming several serves to the ground before Tom had a chance to lift his racquet. The final score was 21-11. Red-faced, glowering, Tom walked off the court. Marty was declared the class champion and given a small trophy. He looked pleased and triumphant. Not even his mother's effusive praise dampened the brilliance of his grin.

An ache centering in her heart, Alison watched him bound over the grass toward Joel, brimming with eagerness to show off his prize. Joel said something and ruffled his carroty hair. Marty grinned and looked up into his face, his heart in his eyes. So much for the tough kid, Alison thought, her heart in her eyes, too. And so much for the tough man. She turned away, unable to watch the camaraderie between man and boy any longer, and saw that Tom was also watching the two, envy twisting his young face into an unpleasant expression. He discovered Alison's eyes on him, grimaced and turned away.

When it was time for the softball match, Joel took one look at Alison's drooping shoulders and flushed face and told her to go and sit on the grass and rest, that he would take care of it. He elected captains and organized the fathers and mothers who were brave enough or crazy enough to risk pulled muscles to join their children in the game. Carefully Joel distributed the adults in equal numbers on both teams. The self-declared umpire, Eve, warned them she would brook no second-guessing on her calls.

Alison collapsed on the grass to watch, wondering where the woman got her energy. What followed was a blessed two hours of something very like peace. The only time her equilibrium was disturbed was when Joel got warm and stripped off his shirt to expose his satiny, tanned torso to the sun. She remembered touching that muscled chest, clutching that hard back in the throes of ecstasy....

At the end of the game, which Joel's team won handily, the group moved to the lunch table Eve had cleared of debris. With great care she brought out the pies. They were all cream pies, lemon-meringue, vanilla, strawberry-cream, banana and chocolate. Two of the fathers volunteered to compete, along with most of the boys in Alison's class.

She was amazed at how quickly three of her boys gobbled one whole pie and were ready to tackle another. A boy named Gerald looked as if he was going to be the winner.

Suddenly there was a commotion behind the table. Tom streaked away toward the lake carrying Marty's trophy. Marty cried out and raced after him, his freckled face beet red with fury and exertion. Joel had been sitting on the ground, his legs crossed, watching the pie-eating contest, but now he jumped up and took off in hot pursuit of the boys. Alison followed. She crested the hill just in time to see Tom race for the dock. At the edge of it, he stopped and turned. "Here's your precious trophy, Shorter. Go get it." With that, he heaved the trophy into the lake.

Alison was suddenly aware that a group had congregated at the crest of the hill and that Tom's vindictive action had been seen by most of the people in the camp. "Go on, Shorter, swim for it. Big man, big athlete. You can't even swim."

In the quiet that followed, Alison heard Joel saying in a low, reassuring voice to Marty, shucking off his sneakers as he spoke, "I'll get it for you—"

Marty grabbed Joel's arm to stop him from kicking off his shoes. "No. I'll do it."

"You're still a fledgling swimmer, ace. This requires diving underwater—"

"I said I'd do it," Marty said through clenched teeth.

Joel's eyes roamed over the boy's face.

"You told me you have to be your own person, define who you are and not let other people do it for you."

"So I did," Joel said softly. "All right, listen to me. You take deep breaths before you do anything. Always a breath first, then let it out underwater. You hear?"

"I hear." Marty sat down on the ground and pulled off his sneakers.

Joel followed him to the dock and knelt with him like a trainer talking to a champion. "Stay cool. Keep your head. Pretend it's a game."

Shoeless, Marty stood up and gave Joel a half brave, half careless grin. "Relax, man. You did a good job teaching me. I know what to do."

Marty turned, grabbed his nose and jumped into the water. Her heart in her mouth, Alison stepped onto the dock.

"He's okay. He'll find it."

Wordlessly she reached out to Joel. He closed his warm hand around her fingers in a comforting hold.

Up on the hill, the waiting crowd was just as silent. Suddenly a woman jostled through the people and trotted down to the dock. "What are you doing what is going on here someone said Marty had jumped into the water but that's impossible he—My God! He *is* in the water. Get out of there this instant Marty you'll drown with your clothes on you should know better—"

Without taking his eyes off Marty, Joel said in the cool, cutting voice he reserved for hecklers, "Lady, you talk too much. Close your mouth, or I'll throw you in after him."

Shocked, the woman stared at Joel. She opened her mouth, closed it, opened her mouth, looked at Joel and closed it again.

A hysterical urge to laugh clogging her throat, Alison gripped his hand more tightly in gratitude. He squeezed her fingers back, and even though she knew his concentration was on Marty, the warmth of his hand was like balm.

How many times did the boy bob up and down before he rose above the water triumphant, the trophy in his hand? Alison didn't know. She did know that when Marty headed for the dock with his inexpert crawl, his red hair darkened from the water, she felt as if her heart would burst with pride for him, and for Joel, too.

"You can swim. You really can—" Marty's mother gathered her wet boy into her arms.

Marty wriggled in embarrassment. "Don't, Mom. I'm getting you all wet."

"I don't care," the woman said staunchly, making Alison's opinion of her soar sharply. "I'm so proud of you."

Eve took charge then, hustling everybody back to the dining hall for a snack and a drink. Then the parents began collecting their children and saying goodbye. Suddenly they were all gone and the camp was empty and quiet. Only Joel, Eve and Alison remained sitting on the benches in the echoing, suddenly too-big dining hall.

"Well, that's it till next year," said Eve, sounding more sorry than glad. Alison moved to help Eve gather up the game equipment.

"Don't bother," Eve told her. "I can take care of it. You take the night off. Go out to dinner. Have a drink. Relax. You deserve it." Her eyes flicked to Joel. "Thanks for your help. It's always nice to have a man around. Not that we really needed you, of course."

"Of course," Joel drawled, smiling slightly.

Eve bustled about, picking up and putting away. Joel put his hand under Alison's elbow to help her slide off the bench, then walked with her to the door.

Outside, in the golden hours of the late afternoon, Joel walked silently beside Alison to her cabin. At the top of the steps, she turned to him. Gathering her courage, she said, "Will I . . . see you tonight?"

He smiled, but there was no amusement in it, only a rueful regret. "I'll be working, and you, if you're wise, will be sleeping. I've kept you awake too many nights as it is."

"Tomorrow's Sunday. I can sleep in."

"I'm not good at goodbyes, sweet. It's best if we say ours now."

"What was it you said to Marty about not letting other people define who you are?"

"I told him he couldn't let other people tell him who he was, he had to find out for himself."

"Do you believe that?"

"Yes, Alison, I believe that."

She looked at him for a long, searching moment. With a courage born of desperation, she said, "Then why have you let your father convince you you're a person who can't love?"

He took the blow without moving, his eyes holding hers steadily, his face impassive. When he said nothing, she knew she'd lost. The game was over. Joel had meant what he'd said about not loving her. She hadn't believed him. The joke was on her. All she had left was her pride. "Are you going to kiss me goodbye?"

In answer, he leaned forward and brushed his lips over hers.

"You're right," she said. "You aren't very good at goodbyes." She turned away from him to go into the cabin, hoping, praying that a miracle would happen and he would pull her back to him, kiss her breathless and tell her he didn't want her to go. It didn't. She walked into the cabin alone, the sound of the breeze in the pines loud in her ears, like someone crying.

Joel stood on the porch, feeling empty. He didn't want her to go. It was irrational of him, but he didn't want to think of her cabin without her there. He had agreed to stay for the weekend shows at the lounge, and while his agreement was loose ended, he wished suddenly that he hadn't been so generous. Yet it was better this way. Much better....

THAT NIGHT, his timing was off. The routine wasn't going well. He sat on the stool the management had provided and wondered suddenly what he was doing there. Memories buzzed incessantly in his brain, memories of words. *You're not a lovable boy, Joel. How can I love you when you don't do what you're told?* And a variation on the tune, with different lyrics. *You've got to get along in this world, do as you're told. How do you expect to amount to anything if you keep getting into trouble?*

He had been as intractable as Marty. And, childlike, he had accepted what his father had said as true.

He wasn't a child anymore.

Alison hadn't accepted that estimation of his character as truth. He had treated her badly for too long, and she had stood on the porch cloaked in her pride, because that was all he'd left her....

Suddenly he wanted to be done and out of there. He clamped down on his impatience and finished his monologue. When he slid off the stool, he was approached by a couple who wanted to buy him a drink. He shook his head and brushed by them. "I'm sorry. There's something I must do."

His face tight with tension, he drove back over the curving road at a greater speed than Alison had taken it the night before. His black mood increased when he pulled up in front of her cabin and saw that it was dark. Had she taken his advice and gone to bed early? No matter. He would wake her. Then he would take her back to bed and see to it that she was glad he'd come.

Crickets chirped a merry accompaniment to the sound of his feet pounding on the stairs. He rapped at the door. "Alison. *Alison!*" There was no sound from inside, no sleepy voice answering him.

His heart sinking, he pulled open the creaking screen door and went in. There was only darkness and a heavy silence unbroken by the sound of her breathing. He was alone.

He turned on the light and saw with searing clarity that the cabin was neat, clean and tidy. The table was cleared, the dishes put away, the wedding-ring quilt pulled up over the bed. He went to a bureau drawer and yanked it open, unable to believe what his eyes were telling him. The drawer was empty. She was gone. The memory of Alison on that long-ago night, picking up clothes, making the bed, self-conscious yet deliciously aware of him, spun through his head, mocking him.

The full import of what he'd done—and what he'd lost—hit him. She had offered him the most unselfish, believing love he'd ever known. He had returned her love by kissing her lightly and telling her goodbye. He had, with his infinite skill at such things and for the second time in his life, driven her away. This time, she was gone forever.

Joel slumped heavily into a chair. In the quiet of the cabin, his body sagged with fatigue and disappointment, but his mind sprang to life. He listened to the thoughts whirling inside his head, his spirits beginning to lift. Along with all the other things he loved about her, Alison had a sense of humor. There might, just might be a way to undo the damage he'd done.

HE STAYED to do the Sunday-night show he'd promised Clayton, but his heart wasn't in it. On Monday, he made arrangements for someone to pick up the rental car and called for the small plane that would take him back to New York.

It was nearly ten o'clock in the evening when he walked out of the airport and got into a taxi. Noisy, dusty, hot, the city impinged on his senses with an aggressive insistence that seemed alien. The bird song and the sighing of the pines had been replaced by the blare of horns and the cry of sirens. He was glad to enter his building and be sealed in the hermetic quiet.

The doorman looked at his unusual luggage with the same odd expression that the pilot of the charter plane had. Politely the man concealed his mild surprise and gave Joel a nod. "Good evening, Mr. Brandon. Nice to see you back."

"Good evening, Miles." He wished he could say it was nice to be back. He was stopping off at the apartment only to touch base with Ted, to organize some cancellations and make his travel arrangements.

The elevator rose with abominable slowness, and he'd forgotten how to put his apartment key in the lock. He'd been gone only six weeks, but it seemed like a lifetime.

Impatiently he pushed open the door—and discovered that the place was ablaze with lights. He stood there, startled, his hair prickling on the back of his neck, wondering if he'd caught a band of burglars in the act. At that precise moment, he heard a noise in his bedroom. Something dropped on the carpeted floor with a thud, and a muttered word followed. He was not alone. Adrenaline flowing, he started down the hall.

A woman emerged from Joel's bedroom. She was dressed in a costume that looked like Hollywood's idea of what kittenish maids were wearing this season, a thigh-high ruffled black skirt, a heart-shaped neckline showing the shapely beginnings of two lovely breasts, a perky white cap and black lace stockings on legs that seemed to have no end. Her lips were lush and full, her cheeks rouged. The only discreet thing about Alison Powell was her hair. Her red-gold waves were caught back and pinned high off her neck. In her hand was a broom.

She looked up, saw him and was nearly as surprised as he. But in a twinkling she collected herself. Her eyes filled with an endearing bravado, she said, "Would the master care to come in?"

Sex symbols didn't develop shaky knees, Alison told herself severely. If only he would smile. If only he would stop looking at her as if she were an apparition. If only he would touch her.

"Only if the champagne is on ice."

She shook her head in mock apology. "Sorry, we seem to be out."

"How did you get in here?"

She slipped her hand into her pocket and brought out a brass object. "The maid had a key. And Tracy knows the maid."

"So you weren't in this conspiracy alone. *When* did you get here?"

"I flew in yesterday." She smiled nervously at him. "On my broom." She lifted it, as if he hadn't noticed it and she needed to draw it to his attention. He almost hadn't. His eyes were too full of her. "It's the 'in' mode of travel for domestics this year, so I've been told."

"Why are you here, Alison?"

"I'm cleaning."

"Cleaning?"

"Yes. Like you did for me."

"I see." His voice silky, he said, "Is there anything else—" a long wait, a pass of his eyes over her "—I did for you that you'd like to do for me?"

"I'd very much like," she said, her eyes flashing, "to hit you over the head with this broom." She shook it at him.

Nothing showed on his face, no humor, no interest, no irritation, nothing. "Come here."

The tone of his voice was not encouraging. She didn't move. He grimaced in impatience. "It's all right. I just want to show you something."

Hesitantly she came closer. He snatched the broom from her and tossed it aside. Carefully, as if her fingers were fragile, he clasped her hand and led her back into the living room, where he'd dropped his luggage. Alongside his round carryall and the attaché case that held his writing sat a green garbage bag. He walked her to the bag and released his hold on her hand. "Look inside."

Alison unwrapped the plastic tie and looked. Mounds of paper balls rustled inside the bag. Her eyes bright, she looked up at him. "What were you going to do with these?"

"Bring them to Iowa so you could throw them at me."

She felt dazed. He had planned to come for her. Joy blazed, lighting a fire in her cheeks and her eyes. "Isn't it lucky you won't have to travel all that way. . . *to get what you deserve.*"

To Joel, those eyes looked chock-full of devilish anticipation. Instinctively he raised his arms, but it was too late. She dived into the bag, came up with both hands full and began pelting him with the paper balls he'd spent an hour making. He stood unmoving. She lobbed several more missiles, scoring direct hits on his chin and his shoulder. She went on firing at him till the bag was empty and the balls were scattered everywhere on his pristine white rug. He let her have her fun, knowing he deserved his punishment. The punishment was not in the harmless wrapped paper she threw at him; it was in looking at her sparkling face and her lovely body and knowing he couldn't touch her. Not yet.

But when the bag was empty of ammunition and she began to scoop balls off the floor to throw at him, he kicked the bag aside and reached for her.

He brought her into his arms, and the joy that had been simmering inside her surfaced. She raised blue eyes alive with laughter to him. "Was it the maid's uniform that did it?"

"No," he said, drinking in the sight of her, knowing he would never let her go. "It was having you walk out on me that did it."

She pulled away to look at him with mock indignation. "I didn't walk out on you. You told me goodbye and—"

"Don't clutter up my story with trivial details. I went back to collect you Saturday night, and you were gone."

Her joy soared to new heights. "You knew then that you wanted us to be together? You're going to let me stay with you?"

He leaned away from her and looked casually into her face, as if he hadn't quite made up his mind. "Just try to walk out of here, sweet, and see how far you get."

Her relief was beautiful to see. She buried her face in his shoulder and said in a muffled voice, "You don't know how much courage it took for me to come to you one more time."

He pulled away to look into her face. "I do know." His face sober, his eyes dark, he said, "I don't deserve you. I'm giving you fair warning right now, love. I'll make a lousy husband and a worse father."

With a fierce, loyal indignation, she declared, "That's hogwash."

"Hogwash?" His smile held a wealth of amusement.

"Of course it is. When I saw how you were with Marty, I . . . I knew that if I couldn't have you for the father of my children, I wouldn't have any. You just don't know what you are, Joel. You're a wonderful man, and I . . ." She faltered, took a breath and said, "I love you."

She was waiting; he knew it. He reached up to pluck the cap from her head and remove the pins from her hair, tossing them to the floor one by one. Gently cupping her chin, he brushed her lips with his. "You're a fighter, Alison, and a believer. You've also got a crazy sense of humor. How could I not love you?"

She felt the words on her mouth, heard the words with her ears. They filled her senses and her heart.

Soaring elation made her tremble. "Thank goodness," she said.

Arching an eyebrow, he pulled away from her. "Thank *goodness*?"

She smiled up at him. "I was afraid that if you decided to throw me out I'd have to tell you a silly bear story to frighten you into letting me stay, and then I'd have to growl convincingly. I've been practicing, but my technique isn't nearly as good as yours, and I—"

His laughter delighted her. When he'd calmed down he said, "So you did know."

"Of course." She smiled up at him. "I guess the joke's on you, my love."

"I guess it is," he said. Looking remarkably pleased for a man who'd had the tables turned on him so neatly, he bent his head to kiss her hello.

Harlequin Temptation

COMING NEXT MONTH

#181 EYE OF THE BEHOLDER Jackie Weger

With her family depending on her, Phoebe was scouting for a place to call home. And she found it. The only obstacle to her idea of heaven was Gage Morgan, who was guarding the gates....

#182 ON THE WILD SIDE Kate Jenkins

Conservative A. Barclay Carstairs and zany Silky Phelan were totally mismatched. That is, until he succumbed to her outrageous charms and ventured a walk on the wild side....

#183 HOME FIRES Candace Schuler

As a single mother, Lily Talbot craved stability for herself and her children. As an adventurer, Grant Saxon lived life on the edge. Lily knew that loving him was dangerous, but irresistibly tempting....

#184 HONORABLE INTENTIONS Judith McWilliams

Jenny Ryton needed a husband if she was going to keep her young ward, Jed. And Nick Carlton was an extremely eligible candidate. All she had to do was make him an offer he couldn't refuse....

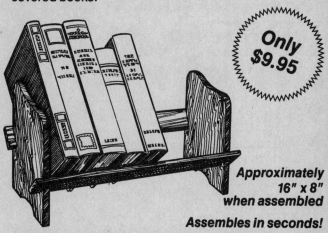